SOS Empowerment Arts & Healing
by Arts Equity Collective

(A Book of Poetry & Visual Arts About Survivors' Stories)

SOS Empowerment Arts & Healing
by Arts Equity Collective

(A Book of Poetry & Visual Arts About Survivors' Stories)

SOS: Empowerment Arts & Healing by Arts Equity Collective

arts
wave
Funding Arts. Fueling Community.

Student Textbook

Title: SOS Empowerment Arts & Healing by Arts Equity Collective
(A Book of Poetry & Visual Arts About Survivors' Stories)
Copyright © 2025

ISBN: 979-8-9991783-0-5
Published by: Arts Equity Collective
Printed in the United States of America

Edited by: Arts Equity Collective
Cover Design: Adam Hayden
Cover Art: "How Do You See What You See" by Jue Amman

About the Textbook

This textbook was created with students in mind. Below the title and author of each poem, you will find themes and content warnings to help prepare you for the topics that will be explored. These poems reflect real-life experiences, often touching on trauma, resilience, and situations many of us can relate to. They are meant to open the door to meaningful conversations and personal growth. Through powerful poetry, dynamic, original visual art, and additional, insightful commentary by MoPoetry Phillips, this book aims to inspire hope, build strength, and support your journey toward healing and self-expression.

As you read, you'll notice certain words highlighted in red. The definitions for these terms are provided below each poem to support your understanding. For educators, facilitators, or group leaders, a Teacher's Manual is available as well. It includes tools for close reading, visual analysis, writing prompts, discussion exercises, trauma-informed resources, and creative tools to help guide conversations and encourage artistic expression as a way of processing these stories of survival. If you are interested in booking creative writing workshop facilitation, books can be included within your contract at a discounted price. Email MoPoetry Phillips at mopoetry@artsequitycollective.org for a proposal.

Dedication

This book is dedicated to you, because you have gone through, or are currently going through mental, physical, or emotional pain. No one else may even know what you face. You just keep making it happen. But you aren't just making it happen; you are going to happen to make it by doing the mental work which starts with seeing things already done in your life. You may have been struggling in school; see yourself graduating. Maybe you are surrounded by dysfunction and division within your family; see yourself surrounded and supported by people who love you. Don't give up! Don't accept anyone else's negativity. They don't have to understand your walk. However, in the end, they will have to accept you are on a predestined path. I'm glad we can walk together through these stories and original visual artwork of survival. Be encouraged, learn to process pain, and find healing through the power of words. Visit https://www.artsequitycollective.org to connect to our survivor community for events throughout the year, and make sure you attend the annual Arts Equity Collective's Survivor's Workshops, Awards, and Ball. Special thanks to ArtsWave, the National Endowment for the Arts, and United Way for making this project successful. Thank you to Shree Phillips & Nedia Mays Magrudger for the countless hours you both put in to help accomplish this goal.

Contents

Survivor Who is Surviving
By Keeley Carrick

(Themes: Alcoholism, Self-Worth, and Healing)

I did not think I was qualified to call myself a survivor,
because I still walk with the pain.
I still fight through it daily, scarily.
Yet, pushing to heal every second of every day,
not believing I was or that I am worthy to put that label on myself.
It's insane. I tried for years to push back what Carl did to me.
What he took from me, and what I allowed him to still touch within me.
It's a struggle I would not wish for anyone.
Was it he who pushed me to the bottle?
Was it he who pushed me to allow men,
and myself to treat me like I was nothing?
I often ponder, why me? Why us?
Then it hit me, IT IS HE.
I give the blame to him, but the healing to God, me, and my therapist.
I am on assignment.
God chose me to go through, so I can get all He has for me.
What is for me is for the world. I am here for you.
Yes, surviving. Yes, learning. Yes, still trying every day.
You want to know the effects of not dealing with trauma? Ask me. Watch me.
It's a struggle getting to the other side. The anticipation to heal.
The goal to find comfort when it gives the false hope of being unattainable,
unreachable, and unsustainable.
You need to understand the effects of relying on a substance or self-medication
to get through the day.
It is me who can tell you a million stories on why this is not the way.
It is me who fights those demons daily.
Sometimes I win. Sometimes I don't,
but I get back up and try again.
Just a survivor surviving.
There is no secret to surviving trauma, hurt, or addiction.
There is no magic spell or secret potion.
It is a daily journey to be a survivor.

Recognize your strength, I say that to you and myself.
The darkest times of one's life can bring light to others.
So, I pass a bit of my light to all in need.
To you, you, and you.
We are survivors surviving.

Commentary for "Survivor Who is Surviving"

I intentionally opened with this poem by Keeley Carrick. It truly speaks to the journey we are on to build platforms where survivor stories can be heard whether it is through our annual Arts Equity Collective's Workshops, Awards, and Survivor's Ball, or through publications like this one. The hardest part of this journey is twofold. First, we have to make people aware that we are all survivors. If you have experienced death or loss, you are a survivor. If you have experienced chronic illness, or you have cared for someone with chronic illness, you are a survivor. If you have gone through childhood trauma, abuse, or neglect, you are a survivor. If you live with someone who is currently battling, or has battled substance abuse in the past, you are a survivor. If you or someone you live with has mental illness, you are a survivor. If you live in a city where you wake up almost daily to news of death by gun violence, face discrimination and racism, and go to school where minority children are three times more likely to have disciplinary action in school than other races, you are a survivor. Furthermore, since trauma is not about what you experienced, it's about how your brain responds to what you experienced, this list is literally endless!

Second, as "Survivor Who is Surviving" explains in detail, many people don't feel they are qualified to call themselves survivors, because they are still healing, or going through recovery mentally, physically, and emotionally. I invite you to wear the badge of survivor! We believe that healing is a continual journey. Good days or bad days, you are still here, and **YOU ARE A SURVIVOR**!

I Am
By Peace

(Themes: Domestic Violence, Empowerment, Healing, and Faith)

I AM
I WAS mistreated
I WAS abused
I WAS abandoned with open wounds

I WAS broken down
I WAS unrest
I WAS trying to deal with the stirring of my flesh

I WAS judged
I WAS discriminated against
I WAS left alone and defenseless

I WAS silenced
I WAS controlled
I WAS scared of being an individual

I WAS targeted
I WAS rare meat at the market
I WAS the blaming topic

I WAS sleeping
I WAS blind
I WAS deaf to what was mine

I WAS striving to survive
I WAS trying just to provide
I WAS stripped of all rights

I AM so Much more
I AM deeper than the core
I AM stronger than before

I AM strength
I AM Faith
I AM ready to walk with grace

I AM Peace
I AM head high
I AM no longer afraid to fly

I AM grateful
I AM thankful
I AM on my knees to praise em'

I AM forgiving
I AM existing
I AM ready to start living

I AM sensitive
I AM salutary*
I AM dancing in all light's glory

I AM ready to tell my story
I AM rejoicing
I AM living in abundance

I AM no longer fear
I AM not in despair
I AM ready for the blessings that's near

I AM audacious*
I AM resilient*
I AM living with fulfillment

I AM more than what they take me for
Thought I would still be grappling on the floor
Living in the times before
I AM the seed grown in the dark

Rising up like a beanstalk
Reaching the highest high
Getting through the lows
This walk alone into self-love is personal
I AM who and where I should be
I AM now loving, accepting, and forgiving of me.

I WAS….BUT NOW I AM!

Definitions for "I Am"

salutary=   focuses on beneficial effects or remedies often even in unpleasant circumstances

audacious= showing a willingness to take surprising risks

resilient=   able to withstand or recover quickly from difficult conditions

Commentary for "I Am"

Who we are is a reflection of the contrast between who we were and who we've become. (Rewind!) In the poetry world, that means to go back and read that again. I invite you to do some real mirror work. Get in front of the mirror and speak over your life. The negative things that tried to define you are your "I WAS." It's ok to speak and say your "I WAS." That makes you honest and transparent. You may need to speak your "I WAS" as the tears flow. Let them flow! Get rid of all the guilt of your past. Then, when you are done, start speaking your "I AM." This is not about making empty affirmations. This is about confirming, manifesting, and empowering yourself to accept who you are becoming. "**I WAS...BUT NOW I AM!**"

Self-Love
By Demontre ThePoet
(Themes: Self-Love, Alcoholism, Recovery, Empowerment, and Suicide)

Take all your shattered pieces & put them all back together.
Through all life endeavors
if you're positive, then that energy can last forever.
In life, it's pretty much a guarantee that you won't always win,
Use the strength you have within to never ever give in.
It's okay if some don't like you for what you say or do,
As long as you push forward and stay true to you.
It is impossible to love someone or anything else,
If you're not at first in love with yourself.
Always have Self-Love.

I learned many years ago,
that pain & love will always go hand & hand.
Stay strong through all that's wrong
& keep spreading love as much as you can.
Constantly push forward,
because progress won't be made moving backwards at all.
Make positive moves through the negative times
& make sure you get up anytime you may fall.
A Strength Within is what resides inside us,
so tap into that potential and you'll go far.
Be the Rose that grew from concrete
- Be the last one standing - be a shining star.

They can't break the unbreakable,
so always be that impenetrable, boulder rock,
No matter if they scheme & plot,
be determined to be a MOVEMENT
that can't be stopped.
Always have Self-Love.

You can smile, but you'll still know tears.
But always be thankful for every breath.
You can be brave, but you'll still know fears,
but still living means you don't know death.
You'll know order, just like you'll know chaos
- you'll know victory, just like you'll know loss.

There's strength mixed in tears,
you may cry, so don't ever give up at any cost.
When you feel stuck
& don't know what your next move in life should be.
When those demons from the past come
& have you questioning if your soul will ever feel free.
Remember your losses can be victories,
if you learn from them & still succeed.
Keep pushing forward,
because we all have people that depend on us
& we all got kids to feed.
Always have Self-Love.

Lately, I've been sitting at home, all alone
just trying to heal from all of my life's pain.
But I don't want you to feel sorry for me,
because I know many are going through the same.
Self-Love is what you must achieve,
because with it you'll have a calm feeling enter your brain.
When you're on the brink of feeling insane,
Self-Love will heal you & once again make you sane.

I was a suicidal alcoholic,
but I'm still here.
- I'm literally living proof that it's nothing to fear.
You can & will make it throughout all these hard
- painful - and trying years.
Just never give in - trust me,
when I say that in the end - you will eventually win.

Just always practice Self-Love,
and connect with the strength that we all have within.
Always have Self-Love.

Commentary for Self-Love

"Always have Self-Love!" Self-love is setting boundaries, because loving someone else should never impose on, or overshadow the love you have for yourself. It means prioritizing yourself even when it is inconvenient for others, or not what they expect of you. It is caring for yourself, so that you don't become so careless that you forget yourself.

Ode to Suga Ray
By John "JG" Gibson

(Themes: Grief, Healing, and Death)

Nothing brings more business than death,
and I hate feeling like I am capitalizing on tragedy.
I try not to think of it as blood money.
But every morning, I know there's a good chance
I will be working with someone in mourning.

Death is an industry.
I have this talent and bills to pay.
I love what I do.
I have to convince myself
that I am no more opportunistic than the coroner.

In my city, I am a rite of passage,
an undertaker with an air compressor.
I put tombstones on t-shirts.
I make memorials for those that can't afford mausoleums.

I am important to the people.
No one wants to be my art,
but no one wants to leave this life without being my art.

I am a cog in the most somber cycle.
It is hard to watch my customers become repeat customers.
Even harder to watch repeat customers become my art.
That is the way of my world.
Accepting it has not been easy.

My people buck (resist) black suit traditions,
because t-shirts hold more memories.
People come to me amidst their worst nightmares,
with open wallets and shaky hands.
Cash is so heavy when it is soaked in tears.

There are museums of my art in broken hearted closets.
My galleries open in funeral homes,
on street corners.
You can see my work at candlelight vigils and balloon releases.

I run a full-service shop.
I am counselor when I'm not being Picasso.
For many, I am the start of the healing process.
This job has made me an expert in the stages of grief.

No one wants to be forgotten when they are gone.
I got to dignify the immortal one
last time by creating an everlasting eulogy.
Not everybody gets to be a corner store mural,
but everyone can be a t-shirt.

Commentary for "Ode to Suga Ray"

Can you name the stages of grief? We talk a lot about loss and grief, but no one addresses secondary loss. Secondary loss is grieving the loss of someone you aren't related to or may not even know personally. Social media is full of stories about teens who have died, because according to the Center for Disease Control (CDC), unintentional deaths, homicide, and suicide rates are the leading causes of death for 15–24-year-olds. Unfortunately, before you graduate you may experience losing a classmate or friend, hearing about deaths of other students at other schools, or people dying within your community. Sometimes it is good to disconnect from social media when hearing these things start to get overwhelming. The empathy the t-shirt press operator in "Ode to Suga Ray" has starts to weigh heavy on him. Although his job helps families and friends unify as they say their goodbyes, he feels it is "capitalizing on tragedy." For him, some days he feels, "death is an industry." Nevertheless, he realizes that he is "the start of the healing process." When art is used to heal, it is a powerful thing.

Playing House
By Yasmin Payne (aka Yaya Wrights)
        (Themes: Grief, Death, Physical Abuse, and Domestic Violence)

My grandmother is dying, and I don't know how to feel. Processing death is always challenging, but processing trauma is harder. I'm not even here looking for an apology, nor am I looking for sympathy. I'm not here with an attitude or any malice in my heart. I don't want to make it hard or make people feel ashamed. I mean, it's insane how a family is like a tree. They are supposed to give you oxygen, but they snatched the air and silenced me. I don't feel right even writing or reciting this. I WANT TO HEAL, but is this the right way? Years of abuse tucked away and hidden. Hatred towards one another. Defaming each other's name. I mean, it's insane. How someone tells you they're hurt, and instead of listening they make it worse. Boundaries were crossed and never put back in. Inappropriate behaviors, actions and gestures became the norm. Instead of correcting it, they would move on. Hypersexuality was just girls being "fast." No one batted an eye, when he stared at her. When standing up for right got you a lash, and people would say, "There's nothing wrong with her." She "just bad" was a common phrase. Beatings were a common threat, and rolled eyes were a common gesture. Playing house was a common action. I'm not here to create problems, ruffle feathers, or interrupt grieving, but my grandmother is dying, and I don't know how to feel. If you don't see a problem with that, then the problem could be you. You were taught to keep your lips sealed and stay out of "grown folks' business." This is more than a curse. This spread to generations. It's vicious. My grandmother is dying, and I don't know how to feel! Your silence meant our suffering. Carrying around guilt, shame, and a messed-up way of thinking. Passing those same inappropriate gestures, behaviors, and actions to others around our age made the world what it is today. Kids need protection, guidance, and truth. My grandmother is dying, and I don't know how to feel. I don't hate you, dislike you, or wish any harm upon you. I WANT TO HEAL. My grandmother died, and it left my Dad in shambles. My grandmother died, and for the first time I have allowed myself to feel. I cannot dwell on my trauma, but now I must heal.

Commentary for "Playing House"

When I was growing up, we lived by "what goes on in the house, stays in the house." What I love about young people today is you were born with boldness. Family secrets aren't safe with you. Does that mean there aren't young people suffering in silence? No. However, once they find their voice, their braveness will inspire and compel the older generation to unify and speak. Thank you from all of your fellow survivors.

"…..the only person with authority to ground your flights
is the woman (man) gazing back when you look in the mirror."
- Rosemarie Wilson (aka One Single Rose ™)

Before reading the next poem, ask yourself,
are you doing anything to ground your own flight?

Take Flight Queen
By Rosemarie Wilson (aka One Single Rose ™)

(Theme: Women's Empowerment)

They try to smother ascension under filthy glass ceilings
conning* queens into believing
we will only fly as high as a king's flight plan allows.
Fake news gives us wings.
I'm coming out.
Manning ticket counters…
Snatching boarding passes…
Canceling departures bearing
archaic* coordinates…
repeating calls for action,
'cause we're not going back!
Sporting my crown, Ace Deuce*…
Ripping runways with style…
Throwing power up
from Soul Plane's pilot seat.
Shattering rooftops at speeds of sound.
Flying sisters out of dodge beyond clouds
into stratospheres where bright stars
bedazzle planet Earth with beauty in the dark.
Soar with purpose!
Don't ever forget diamonds were created to SHINE,
and the only person with authority to ground your flights
is the woman gazing back when you look in the mirror.

Definitions for "Take Flight Queen"

conning=   persuade someone into doing or believing something typically
            by use of deception.
archaic=   very old or old fashioned.
ace deuce= a slang phrase for top-notch or meaning it is the 1's and 2's .

Commentary for "Take Flight Queen"

Self-sabotage is a self-destructive behavior that is harmful or potentially harmful towards the person who engages in the behavior. As you take flight in life, make sure that you aren't hindering your ability to fly by sabotaging yourself. It takes a strong belief in yourself to not only do well, but to shut down anything that can hinder your success. As young adults, you are not only starting to make your own decisions, but you will also be held accountable for those decisions as well. However, age doesn't matter. Most of us fight against falling into the self-destructive and self-sabotaging trap.

You Are Not the Father
By Lamar Taylor

(Theme: Unplanned Pregnancy)

"You are NOT the father!" A phrase that became **synonymous** with ooohhhhs, awwws, and laughter. Embarrassed baby mothers running off-stage just to escape the shame of the camera. We all know the narrative... "Maury, I'm one thousand percent sure he is the father! He's the only person I've been with, I mean, look at him…Look at this baby…He can't deny his child!" Statements which prompt more Maury wise cracks, and even more barbs (insults) between two people who once were cordial enough to lay and **procreate** a seed. The results are in, and for a moment, the audience remains in shock. At least until the next segment...Right after these messages… But what they portray fails in comparison to what I felt the day I received that letter. There is not an adjective, metaphor, or simile I can attempt to put together. That was the only time seeing numbers close to 100% on a test that couldn't be viewed as an accomplishment. Instantly, it felt like my heart was ripped out of my chest. The walls were closing in, and I couldn't seem to catch my breath. Tears were uncontrollably falling from my eyes. Sounds I've never heard came from my depths. It felt like I had just been shot. It was anger, mixed with disbelief, and shock. Flashbacks of the last 2 and 1/2 years all gone within a matter of seconds. The initial fears over time turned to joy. I came to terms as we waited to welcome a beautiful little girl into this cruel crazy world. It's amazing how having a little girl can somehow turn a boy into a man. Well, for some, it can. A whirlwind of emotions, I still remember the sound of her first cry. That almondy sparkle in her eyes. The same one that once lived in mine, which is why she said we favored. But what was once sweet quickly turned to the bitterest flavor. Over time, I'd ask how my Savior could leave me in a position to feel so abandoned. I guess there was a lesson to be learned. There were stripes of being a man I had to earn. Something my biological father didn't prepare me for, but in his defense, he could have never prepared me for this. Therefore, karma did. Now this becomes another story to tell. Another twist in life's never-ending plot. So, the next time you're flipping through the channels, and you decide to tune in, please be mindful of what you find yourself laughing at. The ugly truth is once the cameras go off and those guests exit; each life has been permanently affected.

Forever changed from that very moment, from that exact day, nothing will ever be the same. It's been over 20 years, and I've been reliving that episode, and I'm just now getting around to truly recognizing its wreckage. For the record, life hasn't been all peaches and cream. So, pardon me, if I find it hard to see any good humor in someone else's tragedy, especially when it mirrors mine.

Definition "You Are Not the Father"

synonymous=   same as
procreate=   reproducing or having children

Commentary for "You Are Not the Father"

Many people talk about teenage pregnancy, the possibility of being a single parent, and motherhood, but no one ever talks about the struggles of fatherhood, and what it is like to be a present father when your own father may have been absent. Think about what it feels like from a man's point of view to know that you are having a child by someone you aren't ready to be connected to for the next 18 years. Should he sign the child's birth certificate despite the possibility of being obligated to pay child support even if he is later determined not to be the father through DNA testing, or should he get DNA testing first and then have his name added later? Will he be blocked from visiting the child if the relationship, or friendship doesn't work out? Will he need to go to the nearest child support agency to file a Punitive Father Paternity Complaint, have the mother served with paternity paperwork, and forced to submit to DNA testing to prove he is the father? Lastly, how will he feel if the results are 0%, or 99.99 %? There's so much uncertainty with being a parent. Reread this poem, think about these questions, and make sure you are making wise decisions. Also, visit the Center for Disease Control (CDC) at https://www.cdc.gov/nchs/pressroom/sosmap/teen-births/teenbirths.htm to find out the current teen birth rate in your state.

Wounded
By Anthony Williams

(Themes: Incarceration, Depression, & Healing)

As I limp around in this place,
trying to find my way back to sound mind and body,
fighting to keep myself from wasting away day by day, I pray.
Even though I look fit and strong on the outside,
on the inside, my heart bleeds out of control.
See, only me and the Lord know the pain I feel.
Right now, I'm like a piece of fruit being peeled,
stripped of its protective coating.
Like sand in an hourglass, my pain feels endless.
With the flow of every grain,
it seems like I'm going insane.
My soul yearns for my body to be free,
to come and go as I please.
Counting down time by the coming and going
of the leaves on the trees,
hoping one day soon to be set free.
I know the pruning must be, because if not,
the Lord would come and get me!
I can't help to think how long it will be,
before he rescues me and puts an end to my misery.

Commentary for "Wounded"

Incarceration is a hard process. Intake involves being strip searched which means having your clothes removed and having your body searched **inside** and **out**. For some, even the fingerprinting itself is traumatic. Then, you will find yourself in a holding cell with total strangers. The "bathroom" is located within the cell. Sometimes there is only a short, half wall hiding the area. Other times, it is completely open for others to view as you use the restroom. The food is horrible and even some of the packages read, "Not for human consumption." Also, the smell from the trays it is served on is so gross that it may make you throw up. You are dependent on the correction officers, or CO's for everything, even for sanitary supplies and underwear which are in short supply.

The Veil
By Dr. Kanwal Preet from Chandigarh, India
(Themes: Societal Control, Gender Oppression, Double Standards, and Women's
Empowerment)

The veil, the purdah*,
What does the veil hide?
I often wonder,
The beauty of a woman?
Why the emphasis on the veil?
Does it hide her beautiful eyes?
Or her enchanting smile,
Or those pearly teeth,
Behind those luscious lips?

Or is the veil a symbol,
Of society's insecurities,
Acting as a barrier,
Against the marauding* hands,
Or those piercing, menacing eyes,
That often strip,
A woman of her dignity,
Leaving her scringing*
Veil, the purdah,
From whom?
From women? No, not at all,
For that would be a joke,

For when the veil is lifted,
By women in the company of their comrades,
They compare their looks, their features,
Reveling* in the beauty of each other,
The veil, once lifted in closed quarters,
Allows the women, to lift their heads,
To enjoy the rain, the rays, and the zephyr*
Isn't it time for the men to lift the veil?

Of ignorance and arrogance,
Of hypocrisy and lies,
Of superstitions and traditions,
And other such narrow confines,
That cage women, behind the veil,
A veil that will not be lifted,
But thrown and discarded,
By women themselves,
To let their daughters,
Soar and fly high,
The veil is just a matter of time.

Definitions for "The Veil"

purdah =   is a religious and social practice of veiling women. Not to be
            confused with a hijab which is a type of veil.

marauding = robbery

scringing = screaming while singing

reveling = enjoy oneself as in singing and dancing

zephyr = a soft, gentle breeze

Commentary for the "The Veil"

This poem speaks of the practices of purdah which for certain Muslim and Hindu women it means living in a separate room, staying behind a curtain, or in this case shown in the poem "The Veil," dressing in nonrevealing clothes and a veil to stay out of the sight of men and strangers. This was said to originally protect women. Now its observance is looked at as a religious practice; however, as the author of this poem shows, it is about societal control, double standards, and gender oppression. Nevertheless, always remember not to judge other people's faiths and beliefs.

Always Remember, Never Forget
By MissTee Poetry

(Themes: Incarceration & Depression)

Always Remember, Never Forget
What it feels like inside to be full of regret.
Those feelings you feel when you have no control.
When your heart and mind have no idea which way to go.
When you're trying so hard to hold on to some piece of who you are.
When you look in the mirror and everything
and everyone important seems so far.
Those feelings you feel when you wake up from a dream
of being at the park with your kids or eating ice cream.

Always Remember, Never Forget
Those feelings you feel when you open your eyes
just to realize this cell block is your reality.
You then ask yourself, "When will this nightmare end for me?"
Those feelings you feel when your phone calls go unanswered,
or that pit in your stomach when you don't get mail.
The chaos around you feels like hell.
Another visitation day comes and goes.
Inside of yourself and outside,
your tears you hide before they explode.
You hang your head up or down and cry.
What you wouldn't give for just one more try.

Always Remember, Never Forget
What it feels like inside to be full of regret.
To spend the holidays and birthdays with strangers,
surrounded by brick and metal.
Remembering the smell and touch of one single flower petal.
Those feelings you feel when each day seems longer than the last.
Forgive yourself now, because you can't take back the past.

Always Remember, Never Forget
The feelings inside that break you all the way down.
That made you cry, that made you frown.
Never again let it be your own will,
or pull that takes you away from your freedom and kin.
Just Always Remember, Never Forget

Commentary for "Always Remember, Never Forget"

In the poem, "Wounded" which you read earlier is a male's point of view of incarceration. This poem, "Always Remember, Never Forget" is a women's point of view. However, both are quite similar, because of the regret they have due to being incarcerated, the lack of control they feel, and the need for freedom is so strong. When you are in jail or prison, you are given an inmate number. As comedian Ali Siddiq states it is engrained in your head. You try to forget it, but you can't, because it is something you recite several times daily. Instead of a person, you are reduced to a number.

Me v/s Me
By MissTee Poetry

(Themes: Incarceration, Women's Empowerment, and Healing)

We finally made it through the roughest, toughest part of our life.

I held your hand in high and low spirits until you got it right.

These supernatural events only touch the Chosen as a child.

Then comes the challenges of misunderstandings,

to the street life, and group homes for the wild.

Got through school, independence, motherhood,

marriage, and decisions of divorce.

Jails, probation, misdirected engagements did the most.

Rebuilding to rebuild from scratch due to unhealthy partners.

Various cars, cribs, and plenty of stacks came and went as we were unbothered.

Trips out of this world to stop all doubt in this world and back.

Dozens of deaths and overindulgence led to more attacks.

Relearning our true history came naturally as an explorer.

Leaving paganism and idols alone, the Source directs you further.

Wickedness, corruption, and lies made you sad upon your throne.

To keeping calm, centered, and relaxed, we were forewarned.

Balance in harmony, initiated in weaponry and armored up.

Connected through faith, giving honor due to the greater good was a jump.

Receiving what you ask for and paying attention to your higher voice.

You avoided a lot of paths that would only lead to more hurt.

To applying what you know with recognition and honor

to your needs and wants.

Eating better, drinking better, moving past all who front.

The joy be in our play dates, down time, vacations, and love lines.

Gifts and talents given we proceeded in, because they're mine.

Ventures, bad choices, setbacks, heartaches, and pain.

Look at you now. You're blissful, still soft, but stronger and wiser, not insane.

Intentions stayed passionate, yet, positive and pure.

Determination as you adjusted before finding the cure.

We've reached a level of no regret, fear, bitterness, nor retreat.

I'm here for you and now you came back to me.

As we move forward with our prime selection,

may nothing or nobody sever our embraced connection.

I could tell you one hundred words that describe your **tenacity**.

Forehead to forehead, you already know from the power of **telepathy**.

Here's to the years survived and more to go.

Each step was set where the Spirit can now properly flow.

It's in the galaxy, for its now, for the betterment and enrichment of life.

With you to join in as one of the best in and out of sight.

That was for Me, but I'm also talking to you.

The real come up is doing better with all that you do.

Definition for "Me v/s Me"

cribs=   urban meaning for the word home

stacks=   urban meaning for the word dollar

tenacity=   persistence determination or firmness of purpose

telepathy=   the ability to communicate directly with another person's mind
without using traditional senses of speech or hearing

Commentary for "Me v/s Me"

This poem is proof that no matter what you've gone through in life, you can change. Learn to have faith.

Activity for "Me v/s Me"

On a sheet of paper, I want you to do a "Life Trajectory Map". In order to do so, think of this as a timeline of hills, valleys, detours, ups, and downs. Start at the far-left corner of your paper with thinking about your childhood. As you move from the left corner of your paper to the right corner, imagine yourself getting older. What was life like at 4-years-old? 6-years-old? 10-years-old? Allow yourself to trace the highs and lows of those memories. When you are done, I want you to take a good long look at it. Even though there were lows, there were highs present as well. This visual shows life's circumstances have the ability to change.

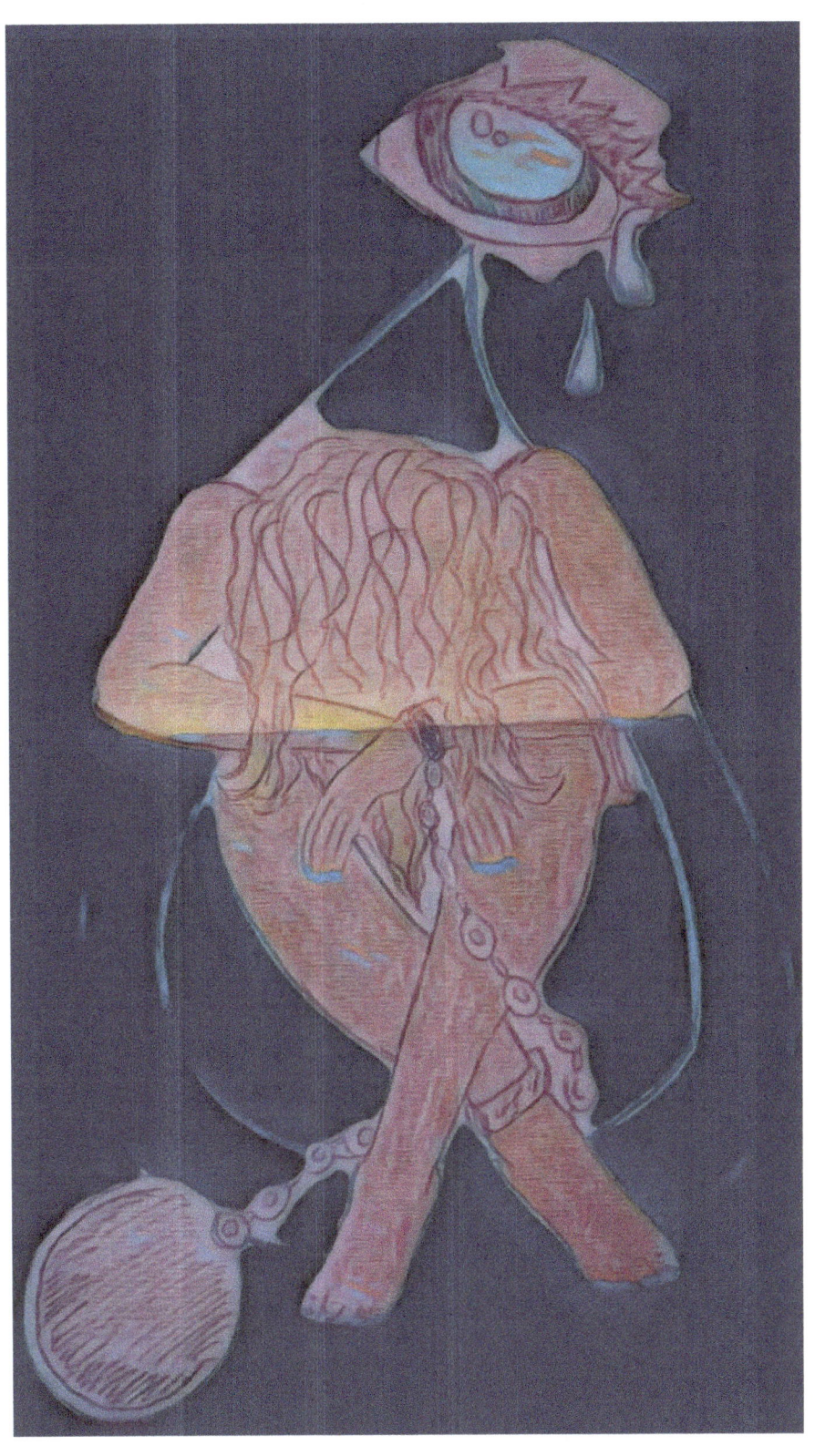

"Me v/s Me" Artwork by MissTee Poetry

Him Too
By Ollie "Hoodraised" Woods
(Themes: Domestic Violence, Physical & Mental Abuse, and Double Standards)

This Feels like an Abusive relationship.
Although bruises are buried beneath.
Still painful to the touch.
Eyes often Fail to see a Harmed Heart.
He is Forced to find peace in an Entrapment of Chaos.
Her tongue spews venomous **Rhetoric***
that erodes the makeup of his self-esteem.
Believe it or Not, Toxicity isn't Gender specific.
Abuse appears in the Form of entitlement.
It's Displayed by broken Promises.
Her committing to the Task of being careful
with his Vulnerability.
Yet, Dropping the ball.
He Asked Was she strong enough to take His Weaknesses?
She Eagerly accepted the Challenge,
but began to make him the **banter*** of her Sister Circle.
It Stings.
She Stings like an attacking Yellow Jacket.
Piercing with precision!
He's wrapped in a White Jacket of Insanity.
Why Can't he Make the Simple decision?
Just Leave!
He Can't.
He Loves Her.
His Abuser.
He's been attached to the Idea of their potential.
They Can accomplish so Much.
Yet, Her, the Dominant, Transforms Theirs into Hers.
Allowing access with Strings that she Guides.
Her Rules.
She Rules with a Stern, Yet, Dainty hand.
Consistently enforcing What's expected of a Man.

26

Still **BELLOWING***, "I've never had a real Man!"

How **Sway***?

When He's bruised Day by Day battling this Abusive relationship.

Him: the King, downgraded to Jester. Clown.

Not with **Jovial Antics**.

This ain't Funny.

Apparently, His pride is irrelevant;

she cares only For money. Materials. Wealth.

More importantly, the Uplifting of herSelf.

While simultaneously, tap dancing on his mental Health.

Abuse. Unseen. Subtle and Effective.

Clean. Accepted by the Feminine. Encouraged even.

After all He's a man.

And according to the Feminazis, A Heathen.

Meaning he should only be treated Low.

Striking for the womanly Cause

Blow by Blow.

If It damages him permanently .... SO!

Domestic Violence only affects Ladies.

Definitions for "Him Too"

rhetoric=	persuasive words that lacks sincerity or meaningful content.
banter=	the playful and friendly exchange of teasing remarks
bellowing=	a deep, loud roar
sway=	a slang word that means "how so"
jovial antics=	happy or cheerful pranks or playful misbehavior
antics=	foolish, outrageous, or amusing behavior

Commentary for "Him Too"

The moral of this real-life story is "Toxicity isn't gender specific." The title, "Him Too" plays on the very popular "Me Too" movement started by Tarana Burke who is an activist from New York City. The "Me Too" movement started as a program for high school students to address sexual violence among women within the community. It ended up being a huge, global movement that helped people find their voice and speak out about rape and sexual assault survivor stories many had held in for years, even decades. Within the first 48 hours that #METOO gained traction, it was tweeted over 1 million times, and there were over 12 million Facebook posts and reactions. It led to a 10% increase in reporting sex crimes. However, still to this day, it is very woman centered. Men who experience domestic violence and sexual assault are often ignored, ostracized, and feel they aren't embraced and supported as much as women. If you are a man who has experienced this, please know you are seen, loved, believed, and supported. There are safe spaces for you to be transparent and heal.

Only 7
By Ollie "Hoodraised" Woods

(Theme: Suicide)

Her face Radiated Innocence.
But her eyes displayed an embedded anguish.
Maneuvering me upon an emotional Seesaw.
I stared into her soul's windows and saw what she saw.
The eldest of the surviving offspring.
They asked if she was aware
Flashback to the night before
Pictures vivid like she was back there.
A 7-year old's nightmare.
She saw blood-stained razor blades accompanied by random splatter.
She saw a sink vandalized by Pill filled Vomit from a failed overdose.
Then tears evolved into a monsoon drenching her face
as she remembered the scene that "Did it."
Graphic!
Explicit!
She noticed her favorite pastime.
Her jump rope tied in Noose form strategically hanging from the vent.
Then she pictured her mother's life source absent.
Away her mother's life went.
Taken by the very object that brought her the most Joy.
Now a self-inflicted weapon, no longer a toy.
A wail released that brought us all back to reality.
She grabbed me as our tears fell gradually.
I know now that she witnessed her mother's Suicide Scene.
She was only 7.

Commentary for "Only 7"

Completing suicide is a very hard topic to discuss. We say, "completing suicide," because "committing suicide" implies that it is a crime as if we were saying committing theft, or robbery. This poem specifically addresses the trauma and post- traumatic stress disorder (PTSD) a child experiences when their parent completes suicide. Some children and other family members have bad dreams, vivid memories, or even false guilt associated with losing someone so tragically. Most of the time, family counseling is needed. Although some people complete suicide without those around them having any prior indication they were struggling, do you know the common signs of suicide ideation?
Please list them below:

1._____

2._____

3._____

4._____

5._____

How
By Tracy "T-Spirit" Stanton

(Themes: Empowerment & Incarceration)

I woke up in Africa.
Had to ask myself,
how did I get here?
Clearly, I flew.
Traveled 5,983 miles.
Entered the Motherland
to execute my mother's plans.
Thank God, that God hands are allergic to erasers.
They say that it was written.
King James made it lyrical.
Nas made it biblical.
My life codified* in Scripture and hieroglyphics.
My oculus* couldn't envision.
Destiny cracked the code.
Would it be too cliche to say that when GOD made me, she broke the mold.
Had to be broken to be remolded.
I'm beholden to the sculptor.
You're looking at a miracle,
an orator, oracle organizing, and mirror too.
I mirror you.
Reflections an automatic response
when performers change forms.
Reflexes,
The objective is connection.
God is the nexus*.
I'm next it.
Footsteps imprinted on scrolls in indelible* ink
I be the abatement* of a death wish
and the answer to a fox hole prayer.
My biggest flex is that I'm still here.
At ten, my mother died of cancer.
Couldn't coddle me anymore.

She loosened her grip on life,
right after she let me go.
She knew that I would soar.
So, I flew.
Became an Avid aviator
Prose, purpose, and pen elevated.
Leveraged the pain and levitated
across nations & stages.
Every fiber of her being that's woven
in every fabric of my genes are screaming,
"That's my baby!"
In this moment, Omen lifted
Don't owe man for flying lessons.
The gift was GOD given.
God shipped it.
Label was postdated, but I made it.
Air freight, Precious cargo
A Little scarred, but overall, **unscathed ***
Ain't afraid of turbulence or tribulations,
even amidst the sunken sullen soulless places.
I knew something supernaturally was carrying me.
Ain't AIR arrogant, but I've Evolved Unapologetically.
Amidst it all, I praised God.
Was a mist of confidence.
Now, I'm drenched in cockiness.
On my cocky **ish*** in the cockpit.
On this charted flight called life.
Creator on the left.
Me Copilot, so I'm on the right.
Somebody done tamed the devil?
My time spent in the wilderness kept me at ground level.
Necessary descent.
Humility absorbed the humidity.
Absolute Altitude corrected my Attitude.
I lived long after the soul's departure.

Hail from the West side of St. Louis
where I'm fluid with the savages,
and flew into Accra and given land in West Africa.
Didn't have to tour the Elmina Castle to know
what it feels like to be captured, shackled.
Literally and Figuratively,
Mentally and Physically,
I've seen the inside of a dungeon.
Spent time in (DOC) Department of Corrections.
This part don't need correcting.
I'm currently living out my life sentence.
Which is why I speak with such conviction.
Persecution got that purpose brewing.
If a cat has nine lives,
I died 8 times, so I could live this one.
We both land on our feet.
A runaway, who found her runway in poetry.
So, when they asked me how did I get here,
I tell them my community strapped on my landing gear and then I flew.

Definitions for "How"

codified=   to arrange laws or rules according to a plan, or system.

oculus=   a round or eye-like opening, or design.

nexus=   a central and most important point, or place.

indelible=   making marks, not able to be forgotten, or removed.

abatement= the ending, reduction, or lessening of something.

unscathed= without suffering any injury, damage, or harm.

ish=   a replacement for a commonly used curse word.

Commentary for "How"

Predestination is arriving at a set place that was determined for you even before your birth. However, predestination is like traveling by plane. We can't arrive where we are going without the departure and the flight. Despite the turbulence in your life (either from things you couldn't control, or decisions you've made) your safe arrival is what predestination is all about. This author shows us the true ability to be thankful for EVERYTHING that has happened. Now repeat after me, "**My biggest flex is that I'm still here!**" Remember, there is a purpose for your life.

Second Chance
By Norman Riggs

(Theme: Suicide, Depression, and Faith)

Looking down on the city,
Sitting high on the hilltop,
Thinking of my life,
And all that's come about.

Never thought it would get to this point,
This all seems so real.
Bewildered and depressed,
Sitting on this here hill.

Feeling empty and hurt inside,
All I seem to do,
Drop my head in my hands
And begin to cry.
These feelings feel so uncontrollable,
For reasons I don't know why.

Knowing I am stronger than these thoughts,
Yet, I feel discouraged, stressed, and awfully weak.
Hard to understand these feelings,
I just want to be at peace,
Sitting here on this hill,
Thinking this would be so much easier,
That's just the way I had it figured.

Pulled out a gun,
Raised it to my head.
Then, I pulled the trigger.

Something happened,
Nothing happened,
It never went off.

I cried out so loud,
Asked for forgiveness,
As I sat on that hilltop.
A voice came out to me,
I forgive you my child,
I understand,
I have more for you to do.

Put your trust, faith
And love in me,
I will help you through.
Never will I forsake you,
I will forever be here for you.

Reach out to me,
Trust in me,
Come and take my hand.
I have blessed you, my child,
You have a second chance.

Commentary for "Second Chance"

Ironically, this poem is entitled "Second Chance." Within this real-life account, miraculously the gun jammed. However, more than likely, someone else may not get a second chance from a suicide attempt, especially one involving a gun. If you personally are dealing with suicide ideation, please notify a family member, teacher, trusted adult within your community, or call or text **988 (the 24-hour suicide hotline)**. Someone will help you do a Suicide Prevention Safety Plan to ensure that all guns, medicines (prescription and over the counter medications) are kept out of reach.

Survival Poem
By Shameeka Shavers Adams (aka Darlin Mikki)

(Themes: Domestic Violence & Children of Domestic Violence)

Blooming, she bleeds, she breaths
Then she breeds and she breeds Seeds
Replicas the resemblance of her
She reminisces on things her mother told her
Stories unfold and she wonders if she didn't have a glimpse
Would this be her daughter's fate
Her younger face stares back at her
As thoughts fade, she wakes to the sound of clutter
She runs to peek, it's her mother
Clashing with hands she knows all too well
As she lies on the floor, the wells of her eyes begin to water
Her lips shiver and move as though she was calling on her daughter
She looks weak as she blinks, praying for strength to brush it off
But the fist she caught came head on
Back-to-back until she was numb
and now she's hoping her little one
didn't get a glimpse....
Years roll by,
Home after home, Daddy was always there
but mommy's eyes were always filled with tears
Daddy always yelled and she disappeared before she was told
Mommy would always end up on the floor...
As time goes on, now she's grown
Baby of her own, daughter old enough to know what goes on
She knows if she lets her see, the cycle will repeat
She peeps the bruises
The contusions that plagued her mother's body
She saw her coming
She watches her stumble and trip over a bottle in the grass
She screams, "No, Dad let her go!"

With the bottle in hand,

A sharp piece of glass to his throat, he doesn't flinch

But from her mother he releases the choke

She pulls away from the grip pleading

Leave him be, it's my fault

Those thoughts slip from her mother's lips

Not meaning, she wasn't thinking

Thinking this would not be a glimpse forever **embedded**

To wherever her child is headed

She dreads the next step imprinted in her

Not sure if her mental is messed up

Wanting to protect her

Walk in her shoes, so she won't have to cover up

No Maybeline Concealer #6

No shade could conceal her

No. Maybe, he'll leave until her wounds heal up

or maybe just kill her with a blow or bash

using only his bare hands

Love? Love ain't gone leave you swelled up

He swelled up to her like an opponent

Moaning and cries for help all she had left

Now, he walks on her future

Making her believe all she sees was it

But she had dreams, so he closed her eyes

Literally, blow by blow blurred her sight

Night after night, no dark knight to save her

Only night turning into days gave her a glimpse

Wishing she didn't fall into this pattern

Ever since her little feet could patter the floor

This is all she saw, but she was taught and told differently

She didn't listen, but she's always listening

Standing in a mirror hoping she won't mirror

She's a mirror image longing to be without a fight

I wish her little eyes would have never

got a glimpse of my life

Definitions for "Survival Poem"

replicas=   an exact copy or model of something, especially one on a smaller
        scale

contusions= a bruise

embedded= fixed firmly and deeply in a surrounding mass, implanted

Commentary for "Survival Poem"

Experiencing domestic violence is a traumatic event. Therefore, it is important to get help immediately to protect your mental health and wellbeing. Also, it is important to get to safety, because children, youth, and teens nationwide have gotten hurt, or even killed while being innocent bystanders of a domestic violence situation. Some children may experience anxiety and depression from constant arguing and fighting. Others may internalize, feel angry, or even physically ill. If you have witnessed domestic violence, try to do things to help you emotionally regulate and reset, lift your mood, and help you process those emotions.

"Homeless" Artwork by Jue Amman

I Remember
By Peace

(Themes: Homelessness, Runaway, Domestic Violence, Self-Worth, and Unplanned Pregnancy)

I remember sleeping in Northside Park's slide
Fear in my eyes every night
Same clothes on for 2 months
Had a room full of clothes and a warm bed,
but wouldn't go home
I allowed myself to be led by my pride
Head too high in the clouds to go home to Momma,
and admit I can barely survive
I remember being the smartest girl in the room
Bragging I had a 4.0 GPA, 2nd smartest in the district
Had a scholarship to go to any school, but I missed it
Missed it giving birth
Missed it working to raise my youth
Momma said, I can't have an education and a baby,
so from school I got withdrew'
I remember having female friends
Somebody I thought I could confide in
only to find out I had no friends
They just wanted to sit in my face
and wait on the chance to sleep with my husband
I remember, I thought I was the ish*
Couldn't nobody tell me nun', cus I was it

Had it all: husband, kids, picket fence, and a dog
I remember coming home and it all was gone.
Being so depressed that not only was my heart broken,
but my whole self felt like it was bent in half
Cus' from it, escaped my other half
I remember going 6 months without looking in a mirror
Telling myself I was ugly, I wasn't good enough

Reminding myself of all my failures

I remember beating up on me

Guess that's why beating up on the next person came so easily

Give my ego, my wounds, my soul a break- I was the catch

You lookin' at me too long and your face I'd break

My daughter's donor punched me so hard

all 6 of my gold teeth fell out in the yard

On my hands and knees in the grass

asking why did you do this to me

Being told I'm not enough and no one will want me, cus' I'm so messed up

I also remember believing that ish

Being broke down and built up

Built up and broke down, built up and broke down

Waking up to my friend's man raping me

Finding out she knew about it

I remember calling the police taking a lie detector test,

a rape kit, and then saying

it's nothing they can do about it,

cus' I'm a stripper and I put myself in that predicament

Catching a charge, cus' I went to her house, knocked on the door, and charged

I remember trying to kill myself with a knife, some pills,

saying I wanna die, but too scared to pull the trigger

Man, I was dumb trying to kill myself for the attention of a ninja*

Kill myself, cus I'm tired of being hurt

I remember when I promised myself, I wasn't going to do that no more

I would always put me first

Daggone memories, I decided to change my life,

not be angry, but try to find the light

Meditation saved my soul, aligning my chakras was my way to mold

Looking at me and saying, while believing, I was pretty

Dusting off that crown I had buried in the ground

I remember spit shining it saying this is for me

I'm willing to take one for the team, because the Team is Me!

I remember when I realized no one from my past could walk my journey,

and come into my present for I had elevated

I remember my spirit guides coming to me saying, "Herbs."
For everything I had went through was part of my position as a healer
I remember I would get mad when they called me a witch
Now, I smile and take my compliment
I remember leaving my body to watch, being scared I might stop the clock
When my guides used to scare me
Now, I embrace them, and we have daily house parties
Just yesterday waking up with a smile, choosing to beat my anxiety down
You will not win today I say, as my feet come out the bed
Elevating my melanated mind, body, and soul, accepting me and all my flaws
I remember my downs, so I can be grateful for my up
My progress can be seen, so I am able to step back and absorb the whole scene
Remembering is what makes me, me

Definitions for "I Remember"

ish=   a word to replace a commonly used curse word
ninja=   a commonly used word to replace a disrespectful word
        that means man

Commentary for "I Remember"

Childhood homelessness impacts students nationwide, so it is very important to be kind to others and realize you may not know what a person is going through. The student in your class, who has problems with hygiene, may have slept in a car last night, or a homeless shelter where multiple families live. In fact, most families are one paycheck away from being homeless. That means one serious illness, accident that requires a hospital stay, unexpected job loss, or family emergency can cause them to face eviction. Also, the lack of affordable housing makes it hard to rebuild after suffering loss. If you personally have, or are currently impacted by homelessness, ask your school counselor about programs like Project Connect which is a school-based program that helps meet the needs of student impacted by homelessness, or UpSpring, a nonprofit located in Cincinnati, Ohio that works to break the cycle of poverty by helping children and families. If you live outside of that area, there should be similar programs in your region as well.

The Village
By Tiffani Reliford (aka Creole Queen)

(Themes: Teenage Pregnancy, Abandonment, & Rape)

"Brenda's Got a Baby," spoke about a New York girl who was molested and impregnated by her family member. It highlights the haunting realities of many living in poverty and facing struggles left to navigate a harsh and unforgiving world. This feels heavy and I can't breathe, knowing there are so many Brendas and Na'Ziyahs who are neglected, unsupported, and face systematic failures. Raised on trauma, so survivor mode is their only life support.

But I take a deep breath and sigh....

My condolences don't feel like enough to Brenda and Na'Ziyah. Even this poem feels like "We," the community, waited too late to address the obvious. So, you ask, what was the obvious? Na'Ziyah Harris, at the tender age of 13, she loved to dance and sing but was too young to understand the difference between love and a grave violation against her body. No one to teach her that those butterflies in her stomach weren't a deep connection with a pedophile. It was an assault against her mind, body, and spirit. If only someone could have helped navigate her confusion instead of labeling her "Too Fast." Paid more attention when she cried out for help. Yet, her story pulled on the heartstrings. Revealed those secrets so many kept in the dark, exposing something painful: shame, guilt, and fear when speaking about sexual abuse, or assault. But, baby girl, it's not your fault. There's a difference between being grown and a grown man **grooming** a child and manipulating you. If only someone would have asked why her small frame showed signs of carrying life inside of her, and why she was vibing a little too hard to a song she should have no emotions to. I can't help but think what could've changed this outcome? If only one adult had noticed, or CPS took action on those 40 complaints against him, what an amazing woman she would have been. I take a deep breath. All my wishful thinking won't change the fact she's no longer here. And as a village, we pretended not to see. We minded our business while this baby endured so much trauma that led to her demise. I can only hope that we can look deep within ourselves to break generational cycles of silence, trauma, and advocate for change, and we can save others like Brenda and Na'Ziyah and be a village.

Definitions for "The Village"

Grooming = Dr. Elizabeth L. Jeglic defines grooming as "Sexual grooming broadly refers to the behaviors and tactics that perpetrators use to manipulate children, their guardians and their surroundings to facilitate the abuse while decreasing the likelihood of disclosure or detection. It is estimated that up to 99% of all cases of child sexual abuse (CSA) involve some elements of sexual grooming"…

The five stages of grooming are 1) victim selection 2) gaining access and isolation 3) trust development 4) desensitizing the child to sexual content and physical contact 5) post abuse maintenance behaviors.

Commentary for "The Village"

In 2025, The National Center for Victims of Crime states 1 in 5 girls and 1 in 20 boys are victims of child sexual abuse. Also, children 7-13 years of age are the most vulnerable. I invite you to share this poem, definition of grooming, commentary, activity, and chart below with your parents or guardians, so that the entire family can be educated to help prevent child sexual abuse. The image "Red Flag Child Sexual Grooming Behaviors: Level of Concern Guide" is from Elizabeth L. Jeglic, PH.D's article, "Identification of Red Flag Sexual Grooming Behaviors." Also, if you or anyone in your family is currently, or has been a victim of sexual assault, please call 911, tell a trusted adult, school counselor, teacher, or call the National Sexual Assault Hotline that is available 24-hours a day at 1-800-656-4673. You can also visit the website at https://rainn.org for more details. It isn't your fault. You aren't to blame. Break the silence and say their name. If you are scared, and want to remain anonymous, call the number for Children's Protective Services in your area. In Cincinnati, Ohio, that number is 513-241-KIDS (513-241-5437).

Activity

Scan here to watch Tupac's, "Brenda's Got a Baby" video on YouTube, and search the name "Na'Ziyah Harris" and write 3-4 sentences about her to prepare for the in-class discussion.

Scan me

Red Flag Child Sexual Grooming Behaviors:
Level of Concern Guide

HIGH RISK

The person increases sexualized touching of the child over time.
The person engages in seemingly innocent or non-sexual touching of the child.
The person uses accidental touching or distraction while touching the child.
The person exposes their naked body to the child.
The person watches the child undressing or while naked.
The person shows the child pornography magazines, images, or videos.
The person tells the child about their past sexual experiences.
The person separates or isolates the child from their peers and family.

MODERATE RISK

The person asks the child questions about the child's sexual experiences and relationships.
The person uses inappropriate sexual language or tells dirty jokes around the child.
The person teaches the child sexual education.
The person provides the child with drugs or alcohol.
The person gets close to the child's family to gain access to child.
The child lacks adult supervision.
The child is not close to their parents, or their parents are not a resource for them.
The person gives the child rewards or privileges (community member only).

ENHANCED RISK

The person does activities alone with the child that exclude other adults.
The person gives the child a lot of attention.
The person spends a lot of time with the child or communicates with the child often.
The person shows the child love and affection.
The person tells the child they love them or that they are special.
The person shows the child favoritism or tells the child they have a "special relationship".
The child lacks confidence or has low self-esteem.
The child feels unwanted or unloved by others.
The child feels lonely or isolated from others.
The child has psychological or behavioral troubles.
The child feels needy.
The person gives the child compliments (family member only).
The person seems charming, nice, or likable (family member only).
The person takes the child on overnight stays or outings (non-family and community member only).
The person gives the child rewards or privileges (non-family member only).
The person engages in childlike activities with the child (community member only).

Interpretation Key:
Enhanced Risk represents behaviors that are 1.68-3.46 times more likely in cases of child sexual abuse.
Moderate Risk represents behaviors that are 3.47- 6.70 times more likely in cases of child sexual abuse.
High Risk represents behaviors that are at least 6.71 times more likely in cases of child sexual abuse.

The Runaway
By Violeta Orozco

(Themes: Physical Abuse & Runaway)

The girl in the movie was so hard you could drop a whip on her.
So hard her skin screamed and tore at the seams,
but she wouldn't squirm at the sight of blood,
knowing the blood was part of the offering.
The ritual was part of the dance.
She held her breath every time he tried to make her cry,
cause' she refused to let him see how hard he hurt her.
Every time she closed her eyes to go to sleep,
every belt in his room would rise and find her
wherever she dreamed she was hiding.
The metal buckle would slash
the surface of her skin.
Every time she felt brittle, she'd remind herself
she'd better make herself hard,
hard like the statues of fugitives she'd seen on the Gulf Coast.
She'd only thought of herself as a ghost
that forced herself to be unseen.
Every time a hand would hover above her head,
she'd play dead like a possum freezing at the sound of any human footstep.
Every step she placed on the ground was a misstep no matter how hard.
She tried to get it right, how softly she tiptoed and made no noise.
Not one boy in school ever noticed her creeping around in the bushes
while they were playing around in the yard.
When she left the house for good, she was so sure someone would cheerlead
her on to lands unknown after all she had done.
She didn't know why no one came to rejoice
with the birth of her newfound freedom.
She wondered why freedom
didn't feel as free as she thought.
She had escaped his house too scared to feel lovely.
Every welt the repeatable proof that any inch that had ever been soft
was crushed and crusted over so many times the skin

became a shell she carried wherever she went.
She took such pride in her thick tortoise skin.
She didn't mind putting it to the test.
She would grind her teeth to powder every day
before letting the mark of the blow be shown.
No sound on her purple lips, no moan coming from her throat.
She'd rather be caught dead on the scene than scream.
She'd buried herself so many times, she couldn't even
come close to dream that she'd be mourned.
She got so good at betraying herself, she wouldn't flinch
when the people she loved refused to move towards her.
For she was hard, she knew no one would ever come
except to beat her.
All the words that poured out of her mouth,
the stories Sherezade* used to serenade the lovers who betrayed her,
only to stay one more day alive.
One more day alert, and running away from houses that melted,
in countries that burned.
Her words were useless to delay the fate
that had been waiting for her in her oldest memories.
Waiting in the stories her grandmother told
before she could even get properly old.
She always knew none of her bones would be spared.
That the hardest part of her body wasn't hard enough to withstand the blows
of an enemy so large she couldn't even see him in her dreams.
She couldn't hear him when he tiptoed into her room,
and only her mouth would be able to move.
Her lightning legs asleep and she knew not what strange spell
could ever keep her from running
away again and again until she jumped out of her skin.
All the rage she had ever felt, would melt and none of the hate
she still felt would rise to the surface in a boiling haze.
Yes, she would melt, for even the hardest metal would yield,
and she believed that the mark the love left was stronger
than the mark any lash could ever leave.

Yes, she believed that the love that she dreamt
was real, was no dream.
No matter how many hoses were burning.
How many countries declared
that a child born on their soil did not belong.
She knew that no matter how long she was chased,
the mark love left was stronger than the mark of any lash.
She'd find a place where she was allowed to exist,
breathe, and be allowed to exist in that sacred instant of peace.

Definition for "The Runaway"

Sherezade = can be used as the name of a person, or a musical place.
> May also refer to a legendary storyteller in "The One Thousand and
> One Nights," often called "Arabian Nights." Also, can be spelled
> Scheherazade.

Commentary for "The Runaway"

Once you get to safety and you are left with the memories of a traumatic situation, dealing with how your mind and body reacted to it can be very upsetting. You may ask yourself, "Why didn't I fight back?" A freeze response can literally make you feel like your hands are tied behind your back, your legs can't move, you go into a shell like a tortoise, you feel paralyzed, and you may not be able to yell for help. This goes beyond fear. It is an INVOLUNTARY trauma response, or way your body responded to the event. Release yourself from any false guilt or self-blame. You are not to blame for something you cannot control.

Activity for "The Runaway"

Reread the poem. With a pencil circle and label any lines from "The Runaway" that shows this survivor's nervous system made them flee, fight, freeze, or collapse.

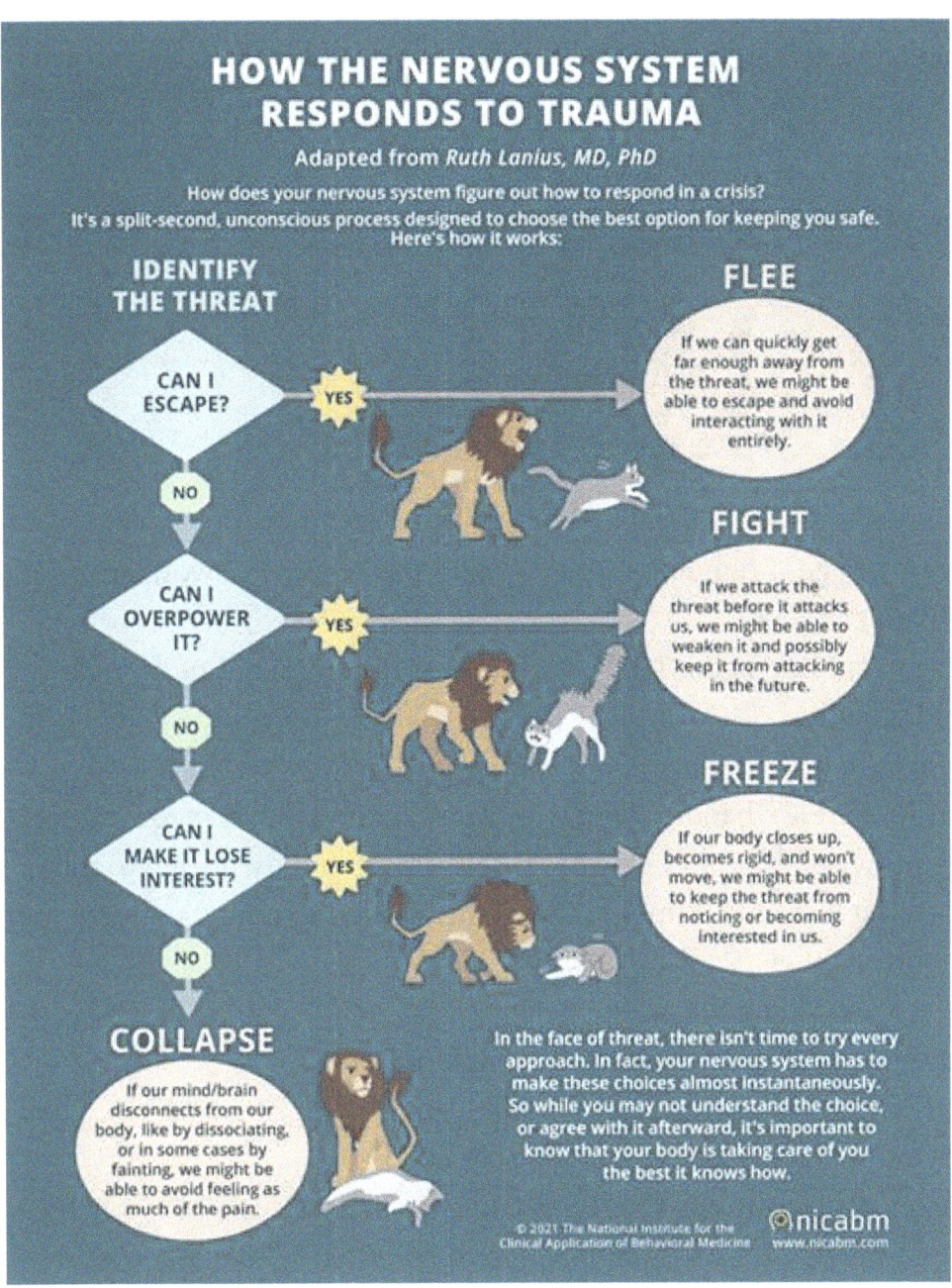

The Suitcase
By Shree Phillips

(Themes: Abandonment & Grief)

Activity: Scan here to listen to a reading of the poem, "The Suitcase" by Shree Phillips to prepare for in-class discussion tomorrow. Write 2 paragraphs about what is abandonment and grief. Discuss how this story shows both.

I had to be 6 years of age. I remember coming into the house and wondering why my Daddy looked startled.
I caught him putting a suitcase under his bed, almost as if he was hiding it.

"Hi, Dad," I said happily.

"Hi, Doll," he replied.

Yes, I was his doll! I loved it when my Dad would call me "Doll." It made me feel special like I was a princess! I think, in a way, it felt similar to how I used to play with my dolls—dressing them up, combing their hair, and imagining they were my children. But wait a minute!

"Daddy, where are you going?" I asked.

"I'll be back, Doll! I gotta go into town," he reassured me.

"Well, can I go?" I insisted.

"No, stay home and wait on your Mom!" he snapped back.

I guess you're wondering why my Dad would leave a six-year-old home alone. It was normal back in the day for children that age to be left at home. We would just sit around and wait for our parents to get home. My Mom worked at Middlesboro Clinic as a dietitian. Thank God for that job and thank God for my Mom's supervisor, Miss Mary Parker. Man! We ate many meals out of that kitchen. We could not wait for Mom to pull whatever she was pulling out of her purse, which usually was wrapped up in paper towels. Ohhhhh, God, it's the pork chops! I used to tell my Mom that porkchops weren't my favorite and that they gave me headaches. I used to love that fried chicken though! You know, I really don't remember my Mom eating much. She would always have her coffee with her sugar and cream. But one thing I know, she always made sure that we ate!

"Daddy, please, I wanna go!" I said sadly.

He replied quickly, "I said no, I'll be back!"

I stood there watching my Dad walk out of the door and head into town. From our house on Worchester Avenue, downtown was about 6-7 blocks from us. I turned left at the corner and continued walking straight, quietly trailing behind him. It was easy to follow Daddy, because of the bushes that outlined the houses along the street. Uh, Oh! He saw me!

"Now, what did I tell you!" he snapped. "Get back in the house.

I said I'll be back!"

With tears in my eyes, I turned around. Memories began flooding back of how my Dad used to let me stand on his feet as he would walk around, while my laughter filled the air. I would scream happily, "Walk Daddy, walk Daddy!" And he would just spin around. "Dance Daddy, dance Daddy!" I would scream louder. It was so much fun, and I felt so empowered! At this moment, I just knew something was wrong. I hid behind the last bush on the corner of our house, peeking out every now and then until my Dad was out of view. Something told me to turn around! Something screamed in my head! But I kept following him. Where did he go? Before I knew it, I was at the Greyhound Bus Station. Wait, is that Daddy? That's his suitcase, but why is he getting on the bus? I paused and watched as the bus pulled off. I looked up at my Daddy as he left, confusion filling my mind. He was on the bus, that suitcase beside him.

As I walked back to the house, I thought, just wait until Mom gets home. I couldn't wait to tell her about that suitcase. After hours had passed, Mom finally walked in, exhausted from a long day of work. I would always try to keep the house neat, so Mom would be proud. My brothers always made sure the fire was burning in the potbelly stove that stood in the middle of the house. Sometimes Mom would come home, and the stove would be red hot. She would say, "Oh Lord!" while she opened up the grate to cool the stove down. "Y'all gonna' burn this house down!" she would yell.

"Mom, Daddy's gone!" I revealed.

"What do you mean, Daddy's gone?" Mom said.

I responded, my voice trembling, "I came into the house, and Daddy had a suitcase. He was hiding it under the bed. He said he was going into town, but I followed him. I saw him get on the bus with that suitcase."

I appeared to have been putting more emphasis on the suitcase at that time, than the fact that Daddy had gotten on the bus. My 6-year-old mind could not comprehend that his entire belongings was in that suitcase and that Daddy was leaving my Mom. I remember my Mom waiting for my Daddy. I don't know who she called on that rotary phone when I heard her say, "Hey, have you seen James?" As the days passed, my Mom started to cry more and more. Days turned into weeks, and weeks turned into months. Months then quickly turned into years. It had finally hit me! Daddy left and is not coming back. And he took that suitcase!

Commentary for "The Suitcase"

Abandonment isn't always as easy to detect as watching your Daddy make the conscious decision to leave the entire family without warning. Many of us have grown up without a father in the home within a society that tells us, "You can't miss what you never had." As a result, we have buried our feelings of loss, rejection, and abandonment. If these feelings aren't recognized, addressed, and healed, we can find ourselves as adults not having much faith in relationships. It becomes easier to leave first than fear dealing with the rejection of being left. That can lead to being overly critical or having unrealistic expectations of others that secretly sabotage chances of friendships and new family ties.

Working to overcome abandonment issues takes continual work and forgiveness. We have to let go of images we hold for others that they may never live up to. That means forgiving others for not being there and not being the person we needed to be there. Forgiving ourselves for holding so much pain, hurt, and for some, even hatred. Healing and forgiveness take time. But you can always tell a person who is on a healing journey, because anytime they could possibly have an opportunity to look at anyone else, the camera view is changed, and they focus on themselves.

Healed Heart
By Demontre Lewis

(Themes: Healing & Breakup)

It's probably because subconsciously there's a fear of being lonely,
but the love that was displayed was far from being phony.
Many of us have issues letting go,
because of the pain that comes from moving on.
The anguish of letting someone you care for be gone.
Those memories stay, but they're no longer around.
You had high hopes, but in the end, you got let down.
Two hearts hurt in a breakup, so don't harp on who's wrong or right,
because you should focus on the fact that y'all no longer have to fight.
No amount of love is worth having grudges and holding on to blame.
Don't let your once calm & cool emotions become heated - irritated & inflamed.

Everyone knows how negative a relationship ending can change someone,
so being positive is the key when a bad ending may come.
Let bitterness be a thing of the past,
the pain of breaking up hurts, but that pain will never forever last.
It just means that a new chapter is upon you,
a chance for you to start over brand new.
You may be stressed and depressed at the same time,
but in times of unrest you're still blessed, so you must see the signs.
It's your moment to just let things go,
it's your moment to just let new things come into your life and flow.

There will be times that doubt will still creep into your mind state,
they'll still be times that you'll feel as if loneliness will forever be your fate.
Love is an everlasting emotion, so don't expect to completely lose the feeling.
Your emotions will go back and forth,
but that's just the natural process while you're still healing.
Hearts never break evenly, so don't compare your pain
with another person's sorrow.
Take things day by day, and just know that with the future
comes a better tomorrow.

Hold on & stay strong and remember better days,
take time to free your mind & just accept the fact
that your life is now in a new phase.
A new journey is scary, but it's normal to feel uneasy,
it's going to take a while before you're comfortable
with a new journey completely.

Embrace the fact that love lost is a chance for a new love to be gained.
Embrace the truth that you will eventually heal from all pain.
Embrace the sunny days that will come after this stormy rain.
Embrace the faith that you had in love,
because the suffering it may have caused, didn't happen in vain.
We've all been burned, but it's just lessons we all had to learn.
Nobody deserves a hurt heart, but sadly with that we've all had our turn.
Have patience - your time of healing has already begun to start.
You are stronger than you know, so breakups will never rip you apart.

Your future will be incredible - your moment is now.
So, make sure you play your part.
Happiness shines all around you & even though it takes time,
please embrace it,
once you have A HEALED HEART.

Commentary for "Healed Heart"

A lot of people put an age requirement on being broken hearted. They use terms like "puppy love" or "young love." To be honest though, the heartbreak I felt when I was younger was the hardest. I couldn't imagine loving anyone else that same way. We spent countless hours on the phone; unlike relationships I had in my 20's or 30's. As I got older, college and working took up so much time that I began to skip over those meaningful conversations. I had more friends later in life, so I didn't have one person who was my go-to with any good news or pain. Unfortunately, I agree with this author, "Nobody deserves a hurt heart, but sadly with that we've all had our turn."

Activity "for a Healed Heart"

Write a letter to someone who broke your heart. If you've never experienced this type of pain, write a persona poem which is a poem where the author steps into someone else's shoes to feel what they have experienced, felt, and determine how that person would react. Although you won't give this to anyone, therapeutic writing is a good way to process through the pain and get the closure you need. Use one of the prompts below to start your poem or letter.

- **Dear____; I'm writing you this letter, because it really hurt me when you…**
- **It hurts that you are gone….**
- **You betrayed/abandoned me…**
- **You weren't worth me, my time, or my energy…**
- **I thought it would last forever….**
- **You betrayed me, and it made me feel….**
- **I forgive you, but I will never trust you again, because….**
- **Having you walk out my life caused me to….**
- **I wish you knew and understood how it made me feel….**

Demise
By Holly "Murder She Wrote" Woods

(Themes: Sex Trafficking & Rape)

The smell of mold
The low temperature of no heat
Dirty clothes on the floor...looking like a bed,
so I don't feel the cold floor against my skin
Suddenly... I remember how much I hate basements
Stuck inside the psychosis in my mind
Remembering exactly what you did 24 years ago
They say time heals all wounds...but that's not true
Those 24 years have done nothing for my healing process,
because tiptoeing down 13 steps, I can smell the basement's cold air
I can feel the pain you inflicted
I can feel your sweaty, dirty hands on the nape of my neck
The knife held tight against my chest
But then, I don't remember
because that's when I passed out
Not physically-
still available for you to take what you came for
But my mind took me somewhere else
as to protect my soul from your brand of evil-
what was broken inside of you
This was not your first act of vengeance
I was not the first girl that you stole from
My body was not the first that you took...
and my soul was not the first one that you broke
You were a man that taught me how to live with monsters
Torment didn't go away when I escaped
It followed me...and found me
Then, it stood in bright daylight watching my every move
Each time you watched me sleep you were raping me inside my dreams

Your disappearance…
or your death has not been worthy punishments for your acts
I can't think of a worthy punishment,
because none comes to mind that are worse than what you inflicted
I can only hope that my strength stayed powerful when I was weak
I hope the night that you tried to steal me back
after I escaped your reality was hell for you…
I hope the day I face you in court…
my eyes burn your flesh
The way your blue eyes always pierced my heart
I may not have been strong enough to fend you off,
but I will always be the woman that stopped you in your tracks
Facing my abuser,
Being the reason for your demise

Commentary for "Demise"

Human trafficking and sex trafficking are sometimes used interchangeably. However, sex trafficking is a category of the broader term, human trafficking which also includes things like forced labor and child labor. One thing I distinctly remember from taking courses in Sex Trafficking is the misconception of how children and teens are abducted. We have been taught for decades to fear the "white truck" pulling into our neighborhood that may seduce children waiting at their bus stops. However, the largest percent of abductions are from family, friends, neighbors or others we know within the community. The person who abducted the author of this poem used their best friend, his daughter as bait. It started from innocent outings with his daughter that were approved by her parents. However, one day after a visit to their home, she was locked in the basement, raped, and barely escaped with her life.

Domestic Violence
By Anthony Arnold

(Theme: Domestic Violence)

You
What are you?
Who are you?
You terrorize your spouse
Beat them down
Thinking you reign supreme

What are you?
So, you think that you're right
Because they return to you
With a misguided sense of love

How can you?
Frighten your kids
Show that it is ok to beat Mommy or Daddy
That this is love

Men and women beat down
Rant and rave
You will do what I say, how I say
Every time I say

Dinner's late...Beat Them Down
Not home when I call...Beat Them Down
Children crying...Beat Them Down
Drunk...Beat Them Down

Violence serves no purpose
Except to hurt and **maim**
Broken bones and black eyes
Scarred children for life

Take a look in the mirror
Next time you strike your spouse
Remember to ask yourself
Who are you?

Definitions for "Domestic Violence"
maim =   to wound or damage someone so severely that it causes permanent
        damage.

Commentary for "Domestic Violence"
It is an unfortunate, known fact that it takes domestic violence victims 6-8 times before they permanently leave the relationship, if they do at all. This causes a lot of frustration for family and friends who state, "Why don't they just leave." However, domestic violence is not a stand-alone issue. There is a progression of violence that includes a web of control, manipulation, and isolation that makes leaving an abusive relationship harder than you think. Most domestic violence victims have been isolated from family and friends by their abusers, so they don't feel they have anyone to turn to for help. Many have been strategically put under economic control, so they feel they can't afford to move out, relocate, or sustain themselves alone.

Some victims feel they are staying in relationships, because of their children. They want to have their child grow up in two-parent home. However, verbal, mental, and physical abuse is not an appropriate atmosphere for relationships, let alone for children to grow. What children witness as a result of growing up in a home where there is domestic violence can cause trauma, depression, post-traumatic stress (PTSD), and other types of emotional setbacks or battles. Many fear that they may lose custody of their child(ren), if they leave their spouse or partner. They may have been beaten down so much verbally that their self-esteem, faith in their own decision making, resilience, power, and voice have diminished.

During those 6-8 times of leaving, and going back, leaving and going back, they have to overcome some of these barriers in order to get strong enough to leave before the domestic violence situation causes their death, or injures them or children in the home. For help, please contact Women Helping Women which is an organization whose mission is to "stop gender-based violence before it begins." They focus on "educating community members and youth about healthy relationships, recognizing signs of violence, setting boundaries, and more." For help 24-hours a day, 7 days a week call 513-381-5610. Website: https://www.womenhelpingwomen.org. Also, our commentator, MoPoetry Phillips teaches classes on "The Progression of Violence" and "Thriving After Survival." To reach her to book a workshop, please email mopoetry@artsequitycollective.org.

D.V.
By Jessica Gaber

(Theme: Domestic Violence & Community Violence)

This man thought he could use me,
Moved in, gaslit, and abused me.
I kicked the guy out, he knocked me down,
Unwarranted violence… excuse me?
After processing shock alone,
Wondering if I should even leave home,
A doctor exam, an x-ray later
He actually fractured a bone.
The next day the cop was a jerk
Saw no crime, only paperwork.
"His attack caused a broken bone, Sir."
He just rolled his eyes and smirked.
He finally took my report
Begrudgingly, with zero support.
The beginning of hope for justice?
Probably not, if it's up to the court.
But the cops won't even try to find him
Because he's homeless, jobless, and hiding.
I had to track him down myself,
Vigilante-style, I'm not lying.
I then waited to see the arrest,
To make sure that his crime got addressed.
In handcuffs, and while being frisked,
The perp actually yelled out, "Thanks Jess!"
He made his bail, thanks to his Mom,
Back to Twitter and Facebook.com.
Spouting off even more
Like he lives in a sleazy sitcom.
I know he likely won't learn,
Since he's only about self-concern.
Acts like he's in a soap opera,
Heard of it? "As The World Spurns"

63

But I keep showing up to court,
"Case continued," hoping I'll abort.
So, he won't be convicted
And can keep straight up lying like sport.
I was prepared to testify
Before a jury, sworn not to lie,
But because it's a first conviction
The prosecutor won't even try.
So now, you're the one who gets a deal?
No matter how the victim feels.
Justice served with a side of misogyny,
How is this going to help me heal?
Disorderly conduct? Yeah right!!!
I didn't report out of spite,
But for there to be a record
Of the crime he committed, despite
The second, and third, and more chances.
Forgiving his bad circumstances,
Never again will pity be
Any part of my romances.
He blamed me for his wrongs,
But was lying all along.
After his so-called conviction,
He put all his lies in a song.
But the only thing scandalous now
Is how people support and allow
Misconduct and community violence
To be the seeds that are plowed.
What can I say, I tried
To disperse the true story, open wide.
So, the next girl he tries to manipulate,
Might see the big picture, wide-eyed.
At least, I can say I have grown
And can now use my pain to **intone.**
The truth of the situation –
Hope for Justice, overthrown.

Definitions for "D.V"

begrudgingly =   reluctantly or resentfully.

spurn=   to reject with disdain or contempt.

intone=   say or recite with little rise and fall of the pitch of the voice.

Commentary for "D.V"

Police and the judicial system are critical allies to domestic violence victims. In Ohio, police can make you feel safe by ensuring that Amy's Law forms are completed on domestic violence cases. The Amy's Law form helps the judge determine the severity of the situation. This form asks victims questions about previous violence or threats, the perpetrator's current level of stress through job loss, reveals the perpetrator's drug or alcohol use, tells if the victim feels safe at home, or if the victim has anyone to turn to if he/she doesn't feel safe. This helps the judges determine final sentencing, and just as important, pre-sentencing protection for the victim such as bond amounts, and electronic monitoring, if needed. Check to see if there is some type of Amy's Law in your state. If not, be sure to make the police, prosecutors, and judges aware of your situation by providing them with the answers to the questions above.

There are plenty of police, attorneys, and judges who do their very best to protect victims. However, as with any profession, there are some who are insensitive, uncaring, and just desensitized to the point that they are no longer able to protect victims of crime. Most victims have to depend on an advocacy network to help them navigate through filing a police report, requesting a temporary protection order, and/or requesting electronic monitoring, so the courts can track the perpetrator's movement, and maybe even relocation services for those in serious fear for their lives.

What's Left Unsaid
By Jessica Gaber

(Themes: Silence & Voice)

I want to say the things I'm not allowed to say.
I want to blow it wide open:
Reality showing, nowhere to run – (Now we're talking!)
No props to hide behind, falsehoods falling to the ground
And only what's real can remain.
I want you to know that I still feel that pain.
Even if you say, I'm not allowed to have it.
Does the blade cut any less deeply, because some say it doesn't exist?
Do my scars not count? Have I once again been dismissed?
Was it all just a dream?
More like a night terror, trying to hold in a scream.
Taking hold in those vulnerable moments
Behind your back, and when your eyes are closed.
Taking hold and putting in roots,
Sinewy and grasping, roots that squeeze the life
From my lungs, my heart, my soul.
A husk, decomposed, I try to shout and –I guess nothing comes out,
That is –nothing anyone wants to hear.
So, nothing gets exposed.
It all gets lost in the shuffle: ears willingly muffled
To the things they want to believe never happened.
The things they want to believe doesn't matter.
The window's been shattered; and to you, there's no issue.
For you can still look outside, I tried the view, but couldn't see
Through all the tears I'd cried.
I want to say the things I'm not allowed to say,
But I hold them in, they ferment and fester
Becoming more putrid with each bite of the tongue.
My saliva swelling and mixing with the drops of blood.
From the words left unsaid, they become rotten, withered things.
Wretched with decay, they hide behind whitened teeth and lies,

And I **surmise** that it's a sick, sick thing to hold it all in.
Fervent and burning, can you look me in the eye
And tell me you're not yearning to feel a little less confined?
I want to say the things I'm not allowed to say, but I don't.
Because the world taught me it's not okay.
That the feelings I have must be defined by my circumstances
Instead of my mind, but my opinions don't come from
Histories, and her-stories, or genealogies
They come from what the world has let me come to find in my own time.
They say today is a gift and maybe the future will be just fine
But all I've got is what's mine and all those things unsaid
Still burning and churning like a **vat** of poison
Haunting me until the day I die.

Definitions for "What's Left Unsaid"

sinewy= resembling the lean and muscular part of a person or animal
ferment= incite or stir up
fester=   a feeling or problem that becomes worse or more intense
putrid =   decaying or rotting
surmise= suppose that something is true without having evidence to confirm it
fervent=   having or displaying a passionate intensity
vat=   a large tank or tub used to hold liquid.

Commentary for "What's Left Unsaid"

There's a huge difference between surviving and thriving. Think of trauma as a car accident. You have survived the car accident, because you are still alive. However, pause here to name some ways you can be injured after a car accident? Did anyone say you could have a broken leg, arm, or concussion? Those are physical injuries. Now pause and think of the mental impact a car accident can cause. What would some of those be? Did anyone say post-traumatic stress (PTSD) or having a fear of driving after experiencing the accident?

When you survive a traumatic event such as domestic violence or sexual assault, surviving means making it to safety alive. A serious determinant of making it from surviving to thriving is finding your voice. Some will need to tell their family, therapist, or friends about what they have endured. If you can't speak about it, at

least turn to the page and write about your experiences. Writing helps move the trauma and memories that are stored in the back of your brain to the front of the brain where processing and healing can take place. It is very important to remember though that it is YOUR STORY! YOUR EXPERIENCE! Try to find safe, unbiased people you can talk to. However, don't focus on whether or not it will be believed by all. As the author warns, "It all gets lost in the shuffle: ears willingly muffled/To the things they want to believe never happened.
The things they want to believe doesn't matter."

Thumper
By Jessica Gaber
(Themes: Domestic Violence, Unprotected Victims, Community Responsibility)

My distrust grew far beyond my abuser.
First, myself, like a hostile takeover-
How could I let this happen?
I thought I knew better! My internal voice starts to stutter.
Looking back, I see from the start the mode of operation he was under.
Seeing me as an opportunity, the memories make me shudder.
Distrust now engulfs the community, their ethics and morals unknown.
Do they see who I am, or just what I can provide them?
Is any of this real? Can I believe what I'm being shown?
But how can they be expected to know the truth
When all that's been presented is a cardboard effigy
Dressed up with lies like lights and tinsel, inflated ego big as balloons
In the Macy's Thanksgiving Day Parade.
A façade of opulence and self-importance, hiding the rotten, hateful core,
The people who don't yet know me can't be trusted to be rational or reasonable.
The people who don't yet know me don't want to get involved or make a scene.
So, I say, to the people I see, who don't yet know me,
Choosing to do nothing is still making a choice-
Is it a good one? Is it the right one? Is it one you can live with?
How far will I have to walk from my car? Are there plenty of streetlights?
Can I count on these strangers around me to do the right thing, if I scream for help?
Or should I hide away at home, keeping my mouth shut like a good victim.
 "Not I," said the bedraggled corpse of my hope reeking
with the death of justice itself.
I stood up and cried out, something WRONG happened here.
With documents and files to prove it, something WRONG happened,
and I hope to Goddess I can help prevent it from happening to someone else.
So, I made my report, I jumped through all the hoops
Back and forth from district to district, court to court, I persisted.
It's not for me. It's for the next one.

The next girl taken' by love bombs and empty promises
Who wants to take away his pain?
I wish she could see what I didn't,
and that when she sees it, she doesn't hesitate like I did again and again.
A quest for revenge, it's not.
You think I get joy from having to re-live the pain,
and the shame our society places on survivors?
The only good victim is a dead one,
because then you don't have to hear about it anymore.
Some say, how will the abuser ever have a chance to show that they've changed?
Showing some remorse might be a start, a public admission, subsequent apology,
Something to show that behind the lying, behind the vainglory displayed
There is something inside — A beating heart.
Then again, believing he had a heart is what got me here in the first place.

Definitions for "Thumper"

effigy=   a sculptor or model of a person

façade =   an outward appearance that is maintained to hide a less pleasant truth

opulence=   great wealth

bedraggled= dirty and unkept

love bombs= an action or practice with lavishing someone with attention or
                  affection

vainglory=   excessive vanity or pride

Commentary for "Thumper"

As the definition states, love bombing is an action or practice with lavishing someone with attention or affection. This is mostly recognized at the beginning of a relationship, but it's deceptive nature can be seen even minutes, days, or weeks after abuse and sometimes is referred to as the "honeymoon stages." What makes it dangerous is that love bombing is normally what is seen by the outside world as relationship goals, having a wonderful, caring, and considerate partner who gives you attention and gifts. This perception helps the aggressors hide their aggressive nature and causes many victims to be blamed or not believed.

My Inflorescence
By Anastasia Shivers

(Theme: Eating Disorder)

When flowers grow through my bones
I might finally feel beautiful
The roses will act as my defense
It's thorns cutting anyone who dares to come near
For I've been told I'm nothing more than a scare
Its petals lure the most gullible into my trap
losing them in a maze without the discarded map
The sepal holding the flower with the daintiest of leaves
to make others see there's more beauty than the often deceit
The ivy will act as my armor
It wraps around the bones that I used to call arms
Weaving in and out leaving trails of grout
It's impossible to remove
You have to choose to see its beauty or its nuisance
Choose silence or its persecution
The lilies will showcase my beauty
They blossom in many
Plenty to go around, but no rhyme or reason to be found
The blooms explode all of a sudden as I once did
Sending everyone else over the bend
Its multicolored leaves are the real thieves
Focusing the eyes and turning them to greed
Stealing what's left to make me think I'm in the lead
My weeds will silence my pleads
Growing through the remains of what were healthy teeth
Remains of what happens after I eat
Being no longer able to spill the lies coming out of my mouth
I will no longer conceptualize what it's like to scream and shout

The daisies, dandelions, and bindweed
will disguise that silence as one of my needs
After becoming a foe to this body
that has been taken over by flowers and leaves
I feel beautiful, protected, and strong
all while wondering why this paradise feels so wrong

Definitions for "My Inflorescence"
Sepal=   small, leaf-shaped, green-colored and outermost part of the flower

Commentary for "My Inflorescence"
There's a reason why Stephanie Covington Armstrong wrote, "Not All Black Girls Know How to Eat." As a parent with two children who have battled eating disorders, I found eating disorders aren't discussed within the African American communities not unlike other stigmas we hold. The big three eating disorders are anorexia, bulimia nervosa, and binge eating disorders. Also, doctors may not be able to classify the type of eating disorder, so it is called Eating Disorder NOS (EDNOS). Other types of eating disorders are avoidant or restrictive food intake disorder (ARFID), pica, and rumination disorder.

Activity for "My Inflorescence"

In addition to studying the "Potential Signs of an Eating Disorder" by Calmerry, pick one of these eating disorders above and write a two-paragraph explanation to prepare for your in-class discussion.

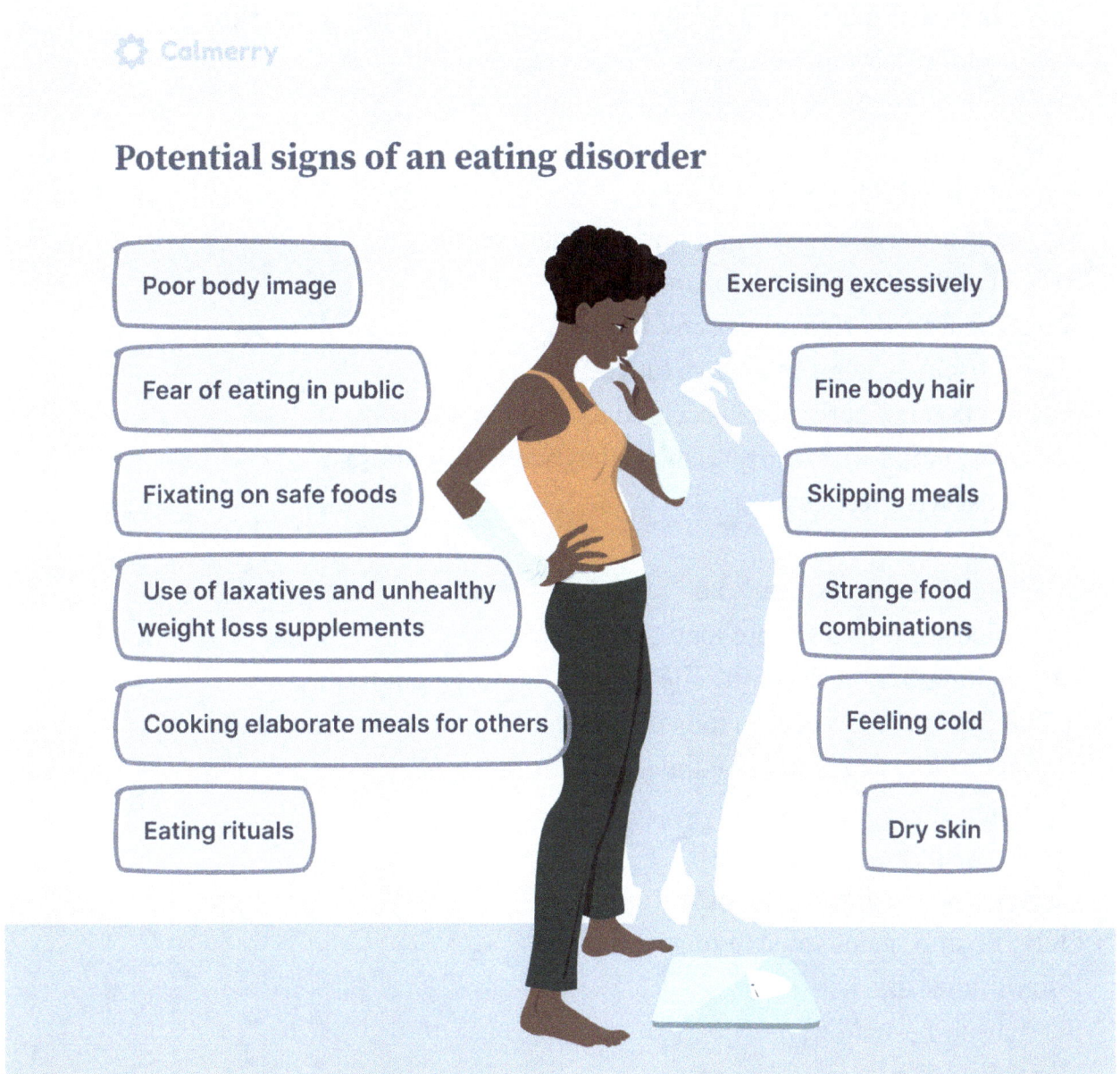

Her
By Anastasia Shivers

(Themes: Insecurity, Body Dysmorphia, and Self-Harm)

I don't look like her
She wears skinny jeans that wrap around thighs that don't touch
The size in a single digit, as if the number doesn't matter so much
Her luscious hair tumbles down in perfected curls
Making her the queen amongst the rest of the girls
And her unmarked arms carrying only her weight,
and not the worlds
My jeans are reduced to that number printed on the tag
Ripped at the knees trying to concede the truth
about the tragedy right above my feet
I have luscious hair, but always tucked away
wishing that my curls were accepted and allowed to stay
My arms, tatted with scars, wishing they were weightless,
or at least weighed less
I don't sound like her
She laughs as the joke isn't her
Her voice sustains a simple tone
Not shaking but breaking the silence and lighting up a room
Assuming the lead vocal in the conversation without any hesitation
My laugh lingers as I act like the joke isn't me
My voice shakes with anxiety
Breaks with impropriety
I lurk in the shadows to let others speak
Only, no one seems to want to speak to me
I don't think like her
She has no hesitation
Her thoughts become feelings,
those feelings become words,
those words become her
She thinks that she's beautiful
And the mirror on her wall feeds her all the confidence she needs

My hesitation is why I turn to desperation
My thoughts become obsessions,
those obsessions become feelings,
those feelings become me
The beauty I possess is just my mess to contain
The mirror on my wall stands tall while sending me to fall
I don't act like her
Because…
I don't know her yet

Definitions for "Her"
impropriety= improper language, behavior, or character

Commentary for "Her"
Whether it is your view of oneself or insecurity from how the world sees you, learning to be comfortable within your own skin can be a challenge. Society has always placed non achievable, false standards of beauty upon us. The age of social media and plastic surgery feed further into our insecurities. How can you compare yourself to those you only see photoshopped and filtered? How can you learn to accept yourself as is, when so many people are getting plastic surgery, tummy tucks, lip injections, and Brazilian Butt Lifts (BBL's)? After you complete the activity below, make sure to look at "A Guide to Body Positivity" provided by Canva templates to see if there are any areas you could work on to be more body positive.

Activity for "Her"
After reading Anastasia Shiver's poem, "Her," scan below to view Billie Eilish's video, "Not My Responsibility."

Artwork & Poetry Honoring Aidan O'Farrell
Prelude by Frank O'Farrell

(Themes: Drug Overdose, Drug Use, Grief, Mental Illness with Drug Use)

"He is a good example of the progression of addiction and co-occurrence or dual diagnosis, starting with an ADHD diagnosis in 5th grade, then later depression and anxiety. He first started taking weed in early high school, then prescription medication. The last two years of his life, it was harder drugs. Ultimately, he passed away from a Fentanyl overdose. He had recently come out of his first and only rehab. His body had no tolerance for such a pernicious drug. I returned from a trip to find him deceased on our living room couch. I believe I may have been the last one to see him alive...certainly the last family member...and first to discover his body. Traumatic for me.

The candle poem is a mix of the paraphernalia I found next to his body juxtaposed with the tradition of Catholic baptism. The painting was Aidan's. He was very proud of it. I made a font from his handwriting. He had a beauty and compassion that I wish more people knew about. The Polaroids are an adaptation of a poem, "All Things Being Equal," by Hank Willis Thomas. Someone once told me that **America is great at responding to emergencies, but often lacks the compassion to prevent them.** I felt that during Aidan's illness, how difficult it was to get help, witnessing stigma, the brutal loneliness of it all...but how my final 911 call summoned an army...too late. Using Polaroids represents our sometimes throwaway, cavalier attitude to the living. The hand imprint is something I suspect is familiar to many students and parents. Aidan had beautiful hands. Who knew that these innocuous, tucked away items would take on such a significance. I need to be his voice now."

Definitions for "Prelude by Frank O'Farrell"

pernicious= having a harmful effect, especially in a gradual or subtle way
paraphernalia= tools needed to store, use, or distribute drugs. For example, spoons, clips, pipes, bongs, etc.
juxtaposed= placed in closed proximity, nearby
adaptation= the process of making something suitable for a new use or purpose
innocuous= not harmful or offensive

"Candle and Flame" Artwork by Aidan O'Farrell

drops of candle wax
near flame scorched foil
with residue
of a stubborn stain
of a final act
left behind
an unblemished soul
brilliant and white and pure
as the spring water
with which he was baptized

Candle and Flame painting by Aidan O'Farrell, 5th Grade
Handwriting by Aidan O'Farrell, November 2022
Poem by Frank O'Farrell (Aidan's Dad)
Dedicated to the memory of Aidan O'Farrell who passed
away from a drug overdose on 31st January, 2023 at age 25.

"Candle and Flame" Transcript

Drops of candle wax
near flame scorched foil
with residue
Of a stubborn stain
of a final act
left behind
an unblemished soul
brilliant white and pure
as the spring water
with which he was baptized

NOTE: The candle is a painting Aidan made in 5th grade and held onto all these years. The handwriting font was made from Aidan's handwriting, excerpted from a journal he wrote in Nov. 2022. I don't have all the letters, caps, and punctuation made yet. He had a candle, wax, and foil next to him when I found his body.

"The Polaroids" Artwork by Frank O'Farrell

"The Polaroids" Transcript

My son a man.
Reduced to fifths
Five fifths a man.
Take the fifth man
Brother
Mother, grandmother
Another brother
Father.
A fifth, a pint.
A cheer, my son.
Six fifths a man.
My son… Amen.

NOTE: This was inspired by the artist Hank Willis Thomas and his piece, "I Am a Man." Aidan was cremated with one fifth of his remains going to each household in our family.

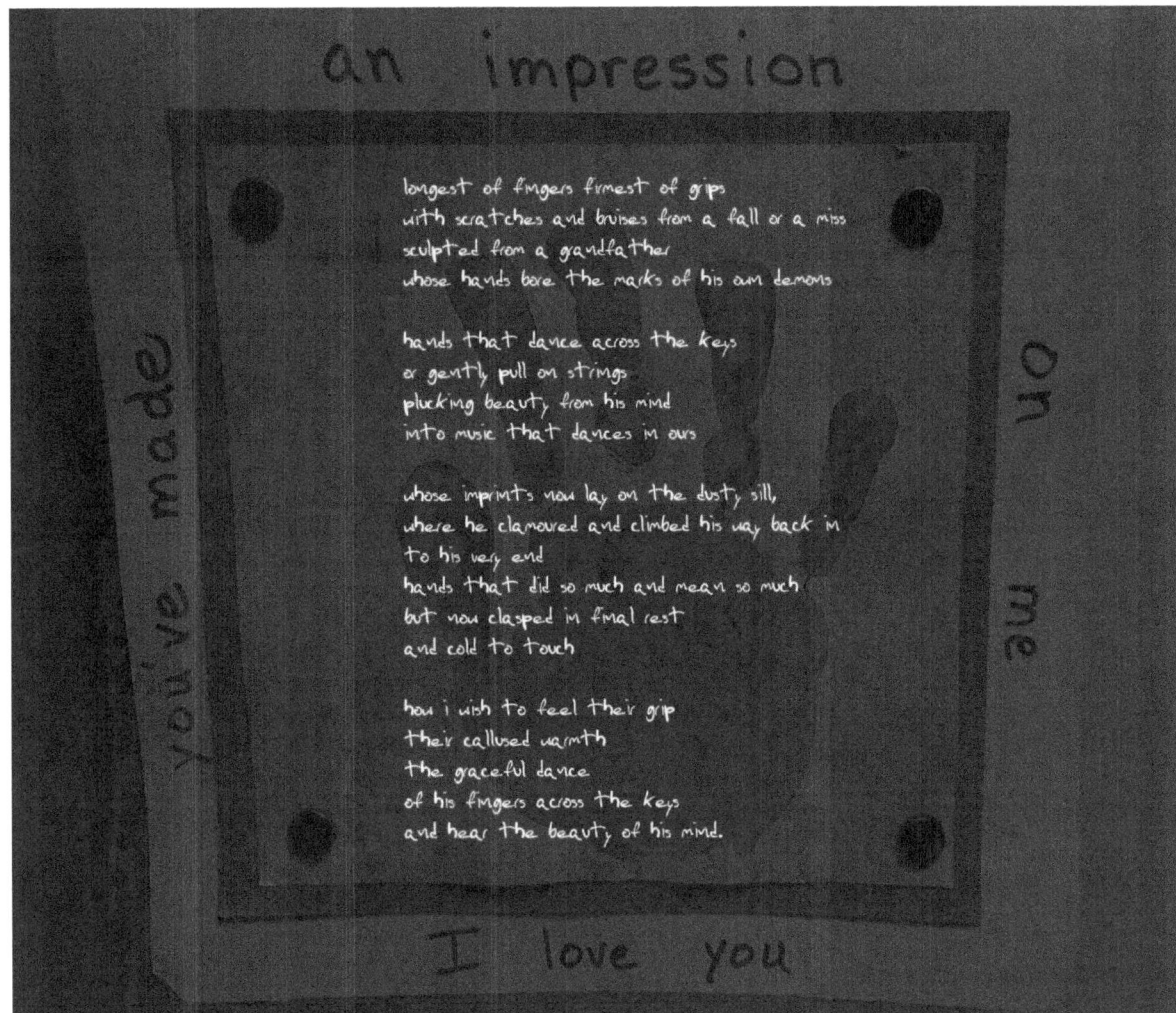

"Impression" Transcript

Longest of fingers firmest of grips,
with scratches and bruises from a fall or a miss.
Sculpted from a grandfather
whose hands bore the marks of his own demons.

Hands that dance across the keys
or gently pull-on strings,
plucking beauty from his mind
into music that dances in ours.

Whose imprints now lay on the dusty sill,
where he clamored and climbed his way back in
to his very end.

Hands that did so much and mean so much,
but now clasped in final rest
and cold to touch.
How I wish to feel their grip.
Their callused warmth,
the graceful dance
of his fingers across the keys,
and hear the beauty of his mind.

NOTE: I uncovered this hand impression when going through Aidan's things. It's dated May 2004. Aidan was 7 when he made this. This poem was also partially inspired by finding his handprints on the window he pushed up to get inside the house. He passed away in the living room later that day.

Commentary for Artwork & Poetry Honoring Aidan O'Farrell

Sadly, Aidan's story is like so many others who have suffered mental illness, self-medicated, and lost their lives to drug overdose. In the 1980's and 1990's, we endured the crack epidemic. Also, starting in the 1990's, many became addicted to opioids due to doctors overprescribing pain medications. As a result, pain management clinics were created to track usage, help better assist those needing pain medication, and ensure proper use and dosage. Despite these efforts, the use of street drugs continued to rise. By 2010, the country began to face a serious heroin and fentanyl epidemic. By the time this textbook gets to you, a new epidemic may be underway.

What I Said
By Anastasia Shivers
(Themes: Eating Disorder, Depression, Suicide Ideation, and Persistence)

When I said I'm hurting
I didn't mean that my stomach grumbled
after eating too much
When I exclaimed it hurts
I meant…
My heartbeat beats in my chest,
waking me up from the nightmare I call sleep
Because it's eat, sleep, repeat
Such a feat to not accept the defeat
When I said I'm sad
I didn't mean that I shed one tear
When I insisted that I felt depressed
I meant…
I felt the pounds of what I call my body
weighing down the legs I just push around
When there's no rhyme or reason to be found
I step down to try to see the solution to mystery
of what we call me and my diagnoses
When I said I'm happy
I didn't mean I jumped and fooled around unintelligently
When I suggested that I felt joy
I meant…
I felt the time bomb tick ticking away
I knew this was the only time I would feel this today
That I could be careless and care less
about what I needed to do and needed to be
Who I needed to show up for
And what needed to see
That when the clock strikes midnight
Cinderella and I's world would fall apart
Reminiscing and wishing the day would not restart
That this feeling of excitement wouldn't fade into the night

Replacing a once feeling of dignity

For the **retributions** of just **succumbing** to **malignancy**

When I said I'm afraid

I didn't mean that there were monsters under my bed out to get me

When I mumbled I'm scared

I meant…

I'm in the dark and can't see what's ahead of me

My future, my life, my reason to continue to fight

My worth, my youth, my unsettled truth

I'm blinded

I weigh my options like I weigh myself

Not with a scale or measuring tape

but with mind of how desperate am I to escape

When I said I'm trying

I meant it…

I meant experiencing the hurt, the happy, the afraid

I will be okay with it

All together or in pieces

As long as my pieces of peace get released back to me

That seizing the opportunity to be the real me

will be appreciated and will be seen

When I said I'll try

You best know that I mean it

Definitions for "What I Said"

reminiscing =   to enjoy recalling past events

retributions=   payment for past suffering

succumbing=   fail to resist pressure, temptation, or some other negative force

malignancy=   a medical context that refers to the state of being cancerous

Commentary for "What I Said"

The hard truth is that sometimes what we are saying isn't what we actually mean. Underneath it all is the same silent calls for help, extreme disappointment, hurt, and agony that are found within this poem. Nevertheless, whether it is listening to this poem, or listening to that still small voice inside, whenever you listen closely, you can hear words of comfort echo back from the cries. The lines that stand out the most for me assures, "I will be okay with it/All together or in pieces/As long as my pieces of peace get released back to me." Peace is the most powerful thing you will ever possess. That doesn't mean you won't have any hard days to face. It means that the peace is more powerful than whatever you are facing. It's what gives us strength to fight and the desire to live. Peace is an internal comfort that isn't determined by your external situations. Say this as loud as you can, **"Release my pieces of peace back to me!"**

As Summer Turns to Fall
By Emma Jackson

(Themes: Voice, Self-Hatred, Suicide Ideation, & Despair)

The September sky laughs at me, and my friends all swear they are dying
My bruised body is healing, but still, all I think about is falling
Happiness is **fleeting**; **indiscretions** last forever
Maybe, I'd be married if I had the right disposition
Evil, rage, and violence live within me like a hunger
Envy isn't green; it's me, if I were a color
I once found heaven in the clouds that now pour rain on me forever
My increasing self-hatred is predictable, and I am afraid I have grown boring
Driven to insanity by my vehicle, these poems
My mouth once held a tongue, then a whip, now nothing
A shell beneath your toes, and sand the water greets the shore
Only permitted to go where the ocean dares to flow
Maybe, I'll stay here forever, real still, and passive
The prophecy fulfilled as the current pulls me under
Sitting in the clouds that only pour rain
The sky was never laughing; it was crying, screaming my name

Definitions for "As Summer Turns to Fall"
fleeting=   lasting only a short time or passing quickly
indiscretions=   behavior or speech that displays a lack of good judgment

Commentary for "As Summer Turns to Fall"
This is what I call a "Transparency Poem." It requires self-awareness, self-observation, and honesty, not only with yourself, but with your readers. The furthest thing from a Transparency Poem would be Langston Hughes' poem, "We Wear the Mask." Digging deep and being truthful is part of healing but be careful. Your own words hit the hardest. Here are a few suggestions before going this deep within a poem. First, make sure you have the necessary trained, trauma-informed support system around you to help you self-regulate and come back to calm after going deep.

Secondly, imagine yourself on a tightrope walking in a circus. You will never see a person trying to learn how to walk across the tightrope without having a safety net underneath. That's why I teach always have a safety net, or preplanned course of action that you know will uplift your spirit. It may be music, comedy, binge watching your favorite series, or taking a walk. Know what you need before you need it.

Lastly, make it a point to recover. Recovering the ball in basketball means you may have missed the shot, but you regain possession or control. Recovering emotionally means even when we miss and have shortcomings, we can give ourselves enough grace to speak positively again, focus on our good characteristics, control our negative thinking, and remind ourselves we are worth loving and able to love. Even if it doesn't seem true right now, what we speak will manifest in our lives.

Gin-Stained Prayers
By Emma Jackson

(Theme: Alcoholism)

I'm the idiot with gin-stained lips, struggling to form coherent sentences, begging God for some grace in the dimly lit bar restroom. They say it's time to go home, because pretty girls don't cry. But they also don't want to die, so I guess we are all blissfully living some lie. The people around me grow tired of my incessant complaints. I am a woman of extremes, prone to wild emotional outbursts. Often yearning for a silence I can never achieve; instead, I drown my surroundings in chaos. When my confidence falters, I convince myself that it's the reason I've never truly known love—I've never been still enough to earn it. I talk myself into thinking that even if love were to find me, I might not recognize it, which is why loneliness haunts my nights. On bad days, I confidently profess that I would barely know love unless someone shoved it down my throat and insisted, I ate it. Surely, I realize this is likely too much for the men who filter in and out of my life, leaving me hungry, forced to confront an emptiness that echoes with voices suggesting my existence would have been easier if we never touched hands. Ah, the thrill of heartbreak, the privilege of playing the scorned woman—the absence of self-reflection allows me to place the blame on you and then act surprised when I still am severed in two, even after five years of trying to erase you.

Life at 27, and the idea of moderation sounds appealing, but I am either afraid of heights or running up the mountain with the intention of free falling. I can't love halfway, and indifference eludes me, so my emotional pendulum swings wildly, never resting in equilibrium. Maybe the history books will deem me as damned and beautiful, but I refuse to portray that woman—the one who pleads for love as if she's guilty of some sin. At least I can feel, so watch me sit with all the beautiful proses I wrote for men who didn't know how to read nor appreciate them, and smile because they never made my words beautiful—I did. They see the heart I wear on my sleeve but overlook the scar on my thumb, the result of countless failed attempts from when I missed as I tried to pull the stitch through. Love has never come easily, but the search for it is always the simplest game of hide and seek. And when I feel lonely, I cry, but not always for myself—rather for the ones who never even try; you're too sad for love, and that's not my flaw.

Not a fan of cruelty, if you need someone to help sort through your broken pieces, there's a spot next to me, and I'll share my needle and thread if you promise to live a little and stop overthinking in your head.

Definitions for " Gin-Stained Prayer"

coherent=   clear, logical, and consistent, especially in communication or reasoning

incessant=   something regarded as unpleasant, continuing without pause or interruption

equilibrium=generally refers to a state of balance, either physical, emotional, or in another context

Commentary for "Gin-Stained Prayers

Alcohol use disorders are serious. People may experience blackouts, shakes, cravings, sweating, dizziness, aggressiveness, compulsiveness or self-destructive behavior, or lack of restraint. It impacts you emotionally by causing extreme highs and lows, guilt, loneliness, and anxiety. The risk and impact for underage drinkers are even greater. The National Institute of Alcohol Abuse and Alcoholism's, "Alcohol's Effects on Health" states, "According to the 2023 NSDUH (National Survey on Drug Use and Health), 5.6 million youth, ages 12 to 17 (21.6 % in this age group) reported that they drank alcohol at some point in their lifetime." The Center for Disease (CDC) says underage drinking can cause alcohol related car accidents, slower brain development, and makes you more prone to violence, including homicide, suicide, and more vulnerable to be sexually assaulted.

Butterfly
By Kimya Strong (aka Silent Assassin)
(Themes: Body Dysmorphia, Insecurity, and Depression)

Beauty of the beholder
But no closure
Within the reflection
Face like golden
But eyes hold rejection
Her mind implies that
She is not the prize
This thought makes her analyze her body
Only to look down and recognize errors
Now the dwellers come to visit
These invaders have no limits
They walk throughout her mind
And come running every time her face turns towards a mirror
A sense of inferiority rushes through her body
Cause depression, brought a party,
And insecurities brought an army
And they disarmed her so spitefully with words
And when they return to their rooms
She's left with unseen bruises and cuts
On her eyes that make her go blind from the beauty they hide
So, I guess you can call her a butterfly

Definitions for "Butterfly"
inferiority= the condition of being lower in status or quality than others

Commentary for "Butterfly"
Prelude: What is unique about the butterfly is that they have 360-degree vision, meaning they should be able to see all around them. However, they lack the necessary organ to see their own appearance, even their beautiful wings. Compare Kimya Strong's poem above to MoPoetry Phillips poem, "Butterfly Wings".

Butterfly Wings
By MoPoetry Phillips

(Theme: Encouragement)

I heard that butterflies don't see their wings. Right around the same time, I listened to a woman say how she admired another woman for her beautiful black skin and almond eyes. When she told her how beautiful she was, the compliment came to her surprise. The woman said, "I was just about to tell you how beautiful you are." The woman noticed she also felt just as surprised. She realized neither one of them recognized their own beauty. This poem is for you.

Dear Queen;
We ignore that we are walking miracles,
who should have never made it.
Life has made us so critical of who we are,
we forget the healing and obsess over the scars.
We subject ourselves to causing our own light to be dim,
when we walk in each other's shadows.
We miss our reflection by keep reflecting on the past,
we turn that mirror that should show us our own beauty
into just another piece of glass.
Our views are skewed, and we have unrealistic expectations.
My dear Queen;
Hold your head up! Quit looking down!
When you look down, it's hard to balance your crown.

Was the Light on, or Off That Day?
By Kimya Strong (aka Silent Assassin)

(Themes: Incest & Rape)

I forgot to turn the light on

I forgot that the lights were already on

It's dark

The lights are on

I'm not safe, wait is there someone behind me

Oh, that's my sister

She taught me that man wasn't the monster

I was taught that some men take little girls like me

Were the lights off when I died in that room,

or were my eyes closed?

Scared to face the truth that my sister

Was the one I feared

Not a man,

but my sister was a monster I'd never heard of lurking upstairs

I washed off my skin; but yet I never felt clean

Am I here, or still in that room?

Days passed me by

Am I still four or am I fifteen?

I'm not quite sure if the lights were on

The bulb always hummed a tone

When I walked through that door she grew near

The one who loved me and filled me with cheer

Told me to close my eyes

Fear my Sister,

Sister, I'm lost in a chill of unanswerable questions

Sister, why are you undressing me?

Sister, I don't like this game!

The reflection of innocence became translucent that day

As I cried buckets of tears, I'd whisper, "I am weak."

As if my body was chained to the floor

She'd make sure that we'd play "dolls"
every day when she got home

Definitions for "Was the Light on, or Off That Day"
translucent= allowing light but not detailed shapes to pass through
                semi-transparent

Commentary for "Was the Light on, or Off That Day"
Memories from sexual abuse haunt many. Our brains have a way of recalling even small details of horrific events: the lighting in the room, the smell of their skin, perfume, or cologne, the sound of their voice, and even their touch. As we fight to heal, things can trigger us to go back to the violation and relive it all over again. Incest is hard to deal with, because these people are still in the family. Depending on the circumstance, we may still see them daily, at weddings, funerals, or yearly at family reunions. Although this person caused serious harm, we get stuck still calling them Sister, Uncle, Momma, or Daddy. However, I remember Tracy "T-Spirit" Stanton teaching a workshop at the Arts Equity Collective's Survivor's Ball. She said that when a person breaches our trust and takes our innocence, they no longer have the privilege to be called by those titles.

Zombie
By Kimya Strong (aka Silent Assassin)

(Themes: Suicide Ideation & Perseverance)

Blood swore my lifeless body to be **enshrined** in the soil.

Every drop not just holds despair, but strength.

The leaves looked on; silent confession pulsated through the roots.

Blood of the fallen, my song deep,

Trees stood under the stars rocking to my heartbeat that once was.

The world turned as I laid lifeless,

I pondered on the vow that was once spoken into my ear,

Untouched by joy nor pain.

It flowed like a flood, mediocrity, and loathing,

Wrapped tightly around each letter and sound.

Yet, beautiful melodies carried on while you took my hand, beckoned me to dance.

With a sly grin, I stood without a single **wince** of doubt.

With every twirl, I felt thrilled as laughter tingled down my spine.

With a chill, he taught me steps,

Where dreams, glisten, yet detest.

With every leap, I learned to soar,

But with every rise, I felt a pretense.

The rhythm hid such a subtle sting.

He found me, found in corners were lost souls meet.

I didn't die.

I didn't want to be the dead friend,

I didn't want to be the dead daughter,

Nor the dead lover,

Or the dead sister.

I didn't want to be the dead cousin.

I didn't want to be the dead classmate.

But our dance made me fragile.

When I misstepped, I broke into a million pieces,

And didn't have the glue to put myself back together.

I was strong, but my heart, my mind, and my body were all so tired.
And you may ponder how I stand here now,
I rose from stale ashes.
This heart that he once pounced upon with **extortion,**
Sparked a flame once again that was wrecked and untamed.
I made a choice to set myself free, cause' the real realization,
It was always me that wanted to die.
I took his hand, knowing his disguise and convinced myself otherwise,
Until I fell to my knees, and my heart **plummeted**.
I was already dead before he buried me in the soil,
My skin was cold before he could even drain the warmth.
In the grip of death's embrace, I blossomed with my **devotion** to still live.
Cause did I ever want to die?
I question… So many questions still unanswered.
The night I fell, I can admit, I did lose the battle.
I lost a part of me that was **exquisite**
When I danced with a friend called death.
But I am here alive.
I might've lost the staggering fight,
But I've won the war.
Reclaimed the life I had left.

Definitions for "Zombie"

enshrined= put an object, or body in a place where it will be protected and
            respected. As in putting it in a tomb.

wince=   to give a slight, involuntary grimace or facial expression
            that indicates disgust or pain

extortion= the act of illegally obtaining something, usually money
            from someone through threats

plummeted= to fall or drop straight down at high speed

devotion=   a deep and enduring love, loyalty, or admiration for someone
            or something

exquisite= extremely beautiful and typically delicate

Commentary for "Zombie"

Struggling with suicide ideation is a dance with death. Death tries to convince us that it is the only way out. The truth is, as this author alludes to, it isn't death we want. What we truly want is to stop the pain of the present that pulls us into this wicked dance. As a teen, your brain is still developing. No matter how mature you are, this can cause you to be more reactive and turn to permanent solutions for what may be temporary problems. Therefore, it is important to let someone know immediately if you are having suicidal thoughts. I don't want you to be "the dead friend... the dead daughter...lover... Or the dead sister." If you need help, please call the number below.

Sinful

By Julie Aubrey

(Theme: Community Violence)

Look at Tamir Rice,
blazing **immaculate**,
something so pure it tumbles your heart,
captures your lungs,
fills your rattling ribcage with nothing
and all eternity.

Look at Tamir Rice,
confident, keen,
knowledge of ages and ancestors,
hidden, braided in his **sinew**,
unraveling, revealing,
rising **aurora** on his golden skin.

Look at Tamir Rice,
mystery, mischievous,
unknown then and now.
love, likelihood of laughter, his art, and words
the great light in his fire eyes
left fallen, unheld.

The curse of this cursed nation,
the **transgression** of this rotting heritage.
But the real sin is when I look at Tamir Rice
I see a similar smile in my now 12-year-old,
and I whisper thanks.

Definitions for "Sinful"

immaculate= something that is perfectly clean, pure, and without
         any flaws or blemish
sinew=   a piece of tough fibrous tissue uniting muscle to bone
unraveling= to come apart
aurora=   a physical phenomenon associated with the the break of day

Commentary for "Sinful"

Police brutality, misuse of force, hasty decision-making, and wrongful deaths are a problem nationwide. In addition, the women who have died by police seem to receive less press, attention, and protest after their deaths. Scan below to hear more about Tamir Rice from Cleveland, Ohio, who was 12 years old when he was murdered while playing with a toy gun. It took police less than 2 seconds from the point of contact with him before he was shot. Had officers taken the time to talk to him, they would have noticed he was just a child and given him a chance to drop the toy gun. How does Breonna Taylor's death, who was murdered in her sleep in Louisville, Kentucky, compare to Tamir Rice? Some fault the emergency dispatcher for not relaying enough information to officers before they arrived to Tamir Rice. What was the mix-up, or negligence that led to Breonna Taylor's death?

SCAN HERE

"You Are Broken" Graphic Poem by Randall Daniels

Grief
By Ari's Bakerys

(Themes: Grief, Intrusive Thoughts, and Anxiety)

Overwhelming thoughts
Anxiety starts coming in the door.
Worried about the things happening
in the world today.
What happens when life goes boom?!
Will there be any more room?
Palms sweaty, breathing almost heavily.
Heart beating faster and faster like a coming disaster.
Hot like a fire burning deep inside.
What happens when there's a coincidence
and almost anything and everything could happen on that day?
That overwhelming feeling inside,
almost like the heavy burdens that ride.
Almost like one being uncertain.
Then you get to stuttering.
It is like the whole room needs some decluttering.
When it feels like all of your **intrusive
thoughts** come about.
Those overwhelming thoughts
may feel like a lot.
Walls start to cave in and those
things that you feared start to begin,
Almost like there is no end.
Then you start to panic and wonder what if.
That feeling of being anxious and not at ease.
Having that fear that something will happen, it's not real clear
Count to 10, take a deep breath and relax again.

Definitions for "Grief"

intrusive thoughts= unwanted, involuntary, and disturbing thoughts, images, or
urges that can appear suddenly. They can be scary, offensive
or shameful and may contradict a person's values or beliefs.

Commentary for "Grief"

Intrusive thoughts themselves can cause a lot of grief, because your mind constantly expects the worst. As a result of these negative thoughts, your emotions and physical body have to constantly process and deal with the "what-ifs." A good way to reign in intrusive thoughts is with mindfulness practices like grounding. One exercise to try is to think of **5 things you can see**. That may involve actually looking around the room to find those five things, or you can pick an imaginary place and think of five things you would see if you were there. Next, pick **5 things you can smell**. Then, **5 things you can hear**. Continue with **5 things you can taste**. Lastly, what are **5 things you can feel**? This simple exercise allows your mind to focus on things outside of your circumstances to calm your nervous system and bring yourself back to the present.

Choices You Make
By Ari's Bakerys

(Themes: Suicide Ideation & Faith)

As I begin writing this, let God be in the midst.
Choices you make can impact your life today.
Didn't know how to describe that feeling inside.
Everything seemed so real.
Attempting to take one's life
almost led to an act of suicide.
Wondered if there was a thing done right.
Tried and tried, but it seemed like
there was a lost piece of design.
Bottled up all those feelings inside.
Wondered why there seemed to be one
hanging on for dear life.
Wondered if anyone ever realized.
Felt like nobody was there.
Depression started to creep in there.
Everything was being placed at the door.
Being in that state for so long.
So many other things started coming along.
Thoughts of taking one's life
lead to attempting to take
that very life that God gave.
That life He died for many times again.
Felt like time stopped and life was becoming timeless.
Wondered what if it would have been.
Felt alone not knowing where to start.
That feeling of being left out.
Without a doubt.
You hold onto that feeling when
the person you love the most goes.
What stops that very person from
committing the act of suicide?

The decision that had to be made.
Thought about what would have happened
if that life was taken that very day.
Would anyone care if that very person
passed away that day?
What would people think, feel, or say?
Now if I may, stand here today,
choices you make, willing to stay not only
for everyone else, but for yourself.
By the grace of God, I am still here today.
There is one thing I can say.
It's always signs and things that lead to that day.
Choices you make, is it the risk you're willing to take?
Choices can make or break you.
Take a look around you.
Ask yourself, do I really want this?

Commentary for "Choices You Make"

Before you look at the "Suicide Warning Signs" chart below, if you or someone you know has ever felt suicidal, what were the warnings signs? Now that you see the chart, are there additional warning signs that aren't listed? Choosing to live is truly the best choice. On average, a person lives until they are 78 years old. Think about how old you are now. No matter what you have experienced in your life until this day, it is actually still such a small portion of your life. That means you have time to heal, grow, enjoy life, make new memories, and have new experiences. Sometimes, all you have to depend on is faith to make it through the darkest days.

NEGATIVE VIEW of SELF

A sense of HOPELESSNESS OR NO HOPE for the FUTURE

ISOLATION or FEELING ALONE

MAKING SUICIDE threats

SUBSTANCE abuse

AGGRESSIVENESS and IRRITABILITY

Suicide WARNING SIGNS

Possessing LETHAL MEANS

GIVING things AWAY

Making funeral ARRANGEMENTS

FEELING LIKE A BURDEN to others

DRASTIC changes in MOOD and BEHAVIOUR

ENGAGING in "risky" BEHAVIORS

SELF-HARM like CUTTING behaviours

FREQUENTLY TALKING about DEATH

Grips of Addiction
By James Wallace

(Themes: Recovery & Alcoholism)

Been in the grips of addiction, so I had to pick my position. Find the interest in living. It sneaks up quick and efficient. You gotta' work for your recovery. You can't just get it delivered- Jimmy John's. Even the sickness is sicker when you just sit there and shiver. Thinking of a way to get you a pitcher, or whatever is your pick of the liter. Nothing against my religion, but maybe I should call somebody and get a different opinion. Doctors don't help either. They just give you prescriptions with your consent to put you in a different dimension. The cycle is vicious like you're better off sitting in prison. The price for your admission is just your attention to take a sit down and listen. I remember sipping my liquor trying to envision a picture, being a manageable addict while giving the waitress tips for a pitcher.

Commentary for "Grips of Addiction"
Even Jimmy Johns had to stop using the advertisement, "Freaky Fast," because it was claimed that this slogan caused a driver to drive so fast and reckless that it caused a serious accident. Recovery from drugs and alcohol is something that also can't be done fast. There aren't any quick fixes. In fact, most treatment centers teach that, "Once an addict, always an addict." This points to the destructive nature of addiction which keeps people in a lifetime of recovery and should be an encouragement to avoid drugs and alcohol use.

Light in the Dark
By Tiera Porter-House

(Theme: Healing)

This healing didn't come without darkness.
The hidden unknown boundaries that kept me from breaking free.
The false sense of safety that I thought was saving me,
but was actually caving me deeper inside of my own mind.
My own emotions, hurt feelings left unspoken,
I was chokin' to say, "I played a part in the drama."
Before it manifested into reality,
the thoughts of unkind people played over and over again in my mind,
and so that became the sequel for every next scene.
I anticipated the disappointment just to say, "I knew it."
Not even knowing that I didn't know that
my mind and hurt emotions were prewriting the script
for my subconscious to play out.
I was unaware.
Scared, tired of being overlooked,
and overused for being so rare.
After a while,
I expected it, and accepted misuse as truth.
This light, this healing, didn't come without darkness.
And darkness still did and is doing its divine duty.
And bringing and brought me back to the light.

Commentary for "Light in the Dark"

Taking accountability is a true sign of maturity. Tiera Porter-House says, "I was chokin' to say, "I played a part in the drama." There are three parts of a story: their version, your version, and normally somewhere in between which is the truth. Allow yourself to look for chances to admit when you are wrong and think about different decisions you could have made to have better outcomes. It's a way to bring light into the darkness.

Some Stuff
By Mary Reid

(Themes: Unplanned Pregnancy & Grief)

I don't talk about it often
And don't let this smile fool you
I've been through some stuff
I loved a boy and
because we didn't wait
A baby we did create
We were scared and didn't want to tell our parents
We took the easy way out
It's a decision I still think a lot about
I've been thru' some stuff
So don't let my smile fool ya'
That boy and I, we tried marriage, but he didn't Understand
his hands were not supposed to be around my neck
Oh, I've been thru' some stuff
Don't let this smile fool ya'
I have been a Single parent
With bills that couldn't get paid
Mommy and Daddy now both gone
Grief lives with me everyday
But I have learned the way
To get through my stuff
This smile is my stance
Because the one who has carried Me
brings me such joy
That this smile is His gift to you
To show that you can make it through too.

Commentary for "Some Stuff"

A few poems within this publication have addressed domestic violence. This one addresses an even more serious type of physical abuse which is strangulation. The Ohio Domestic Violence Network (ODVN) states that if your partner strangles you, you are seven times more likely to be killed by them. It is best to get out as soon as you can. Plan your escape! Do not confront the person or notify them that you are planning to leave, because that greatly increases the risk of death as well. In Ohio, from July 1, 2023, to June 30, 2024, there were 114 deaths due to domestic violence which included 79 victims and 35 perpetrators. Leaving an abusive person truly may save your life.

Love Hurts, Love Heals
By NOC Giant

(Theme: Healing)

She loved unconditionally
Her heart was an open book
Anyone with time could read it
A giver of her mind, body, and soul
Fueled with emotional passion
She came with outstretched arms
Until they took without return of what she gave
Ripped her book to shreds and darkened her soul
Tortured her body and **ravaged** her mind
The tears burned her flesh
The pain bruised her heart
She clutched her arms to her body
Crossed at the stomach from **agony**
Her smile now down
No balance of emotion
Simply a wrecked love coaster
The desire to feel such again
Was a feeling undesired
Her arms cross and fold at the elbows now
Distrust of them runs like toxins through her veins
She only sees them by a troubled past
They call her mad
It is said that love conquers all, and now she is its prisoner
For now, her arms cross around her neck on the shoulders…
Only wanting to be held by them
Frozen in whimpers and bruised by her past
She only can cry herself to sleep nowadays
Alone is she
Dampened face, in a fetal position
Her only rescue is her outstretched arms
An invitation of love to strangers with agendas not of her own
Hoping that someone will open their book of love just as she had

Definitions for "Love Hurts, Love Heals"

ravaged= severely damaged, devastated

agony=   extreme physical or mental suffering

Commentary for "Love Hurts, Love Heals"

Love is part of Maslow's basic needs. When we are born, it is so important to be loved that babies who don't get embraced and held can literally die. In fact, if a baby is abandoned, the hospital staff will use volunteers to come just to hold the baby and show them love. Love is healing! As we grow older, we fail to realize how important it is to be loved. Despite showing love in other ways, some of us may have grown up within families that don't say I love you. We may not be used to being hugged. When we grow up and have our own families, it is important to change those cycles of behavior. We may need counseling. We may need to hang around peers and friends whose families are more loving in order to see real love in action.

Activity for "Love Hurts, Love Heals"

Create a List Poem of 20 things that will make you feel loved. After your List Poem is complete, look at how many things aren't tangible materials, or things that can be bought. Love (truly), Don't Cost a Thing!

Balancing Before the Break
By Michee- Madonna

(Themes: Boundaries & Verbal Abuse)

I teetered into frame
all wobbly and misshaped
A blurred mystique of the person I used to be.

Scales off,
weighted mistakes…
ahhh, the turns we take.

I hung down and swung into a pendulum,
a pickaxe tapped
mental metal formations
manipulated me malleable
for another's sake.

I believe I crossed over to do a backflip,
and sprung rejuvenated off a diving board.
Oh, I wish it was that easy!

See, I splashed belly full of flip-flops.
I tapped noisily to break the fall.
I wished a swan featured in this whirlwind
of a duckling in this suckling pool of collected tears!

See, paddling is a must.
To rest doggedly up against sanity.
These strides will snap and adjust clean lines wavering above tides.
Bobbing buoys of goodbyes.
Letting go of the raft of rallying wraith

Shadows tilted to noon,
I'm left barely a person
a stature, weightless lagoon.
I've been making floating my saving…

Whilst facing the moon.
Bared my soul,
howling & wandering to gain it back.
As I ingested toxins unfiltered,
no goggles or swim caps,
I spit out words of abuse
Which almost sunk me.

To think,
the task was just to stay above water.
To make it back to land.
To walk on my own two feet.

But the distraction before the break,
guns blaring
pop, go, race,
stammered me, held me tethered too,
tight teeth turned to slighted bites of frustration.

Just trying to remember…
if opposite leg kicks are mandatory
as you cup water overhead,
and away from covering you.
And if Continuing
is called swimming.

See, Laps in love are depending on you navigating.
I'll be fishing for a better formation
of handling me before picking
when the time's right.
And if balancing a new line will cast better,
I needed just a line of mine
to balance before the break.

Definitions for "Balancing Before the Break"

mystique =	a fascinating aura of mystery, awe, and power surrounding someone or something
pendulum=	a weight hung from a fixed point
manipulated=	handle or control
malleable=	of a metal or other material able to be hammered or pressed permanently without breaking or cracking
rejuvenated=	having been given new energy or vigor, energized
suckling=	an unweaned child or animal
doggedly=	in a matter that shows tenacity or persistence
buoys=	an anchor float serving as a navigation mark to show reefs or other hazards
wraith=	a ghost or ghostlike image of someone, especially one seen shortly before or after their death
lagoon=	a stretch of saltwater separated from the sea by a low sandbank or coral reef
stammered=	to speak with sudden involuntary pauses and a tendency to repeat the initial letters of words. Also, it can mean a stuttered or jolted stop or pause in movement
tethered too=	to be excessively attached to something or someone to the point of restriction or dependence

Commentary of "Balancing Before the Break"

The overall moral of the story or theme of this poem is to avoid being "tethered too" anyone. The definition above says "tethered too" is to be excessively attached to something or someone to the point of restriction or dependence. When you fail to set boundaries, you can easily end up in relationships that are wrong attachments. Whether you are a young man or young woman, I always caution to test the waters. There are certain things we can do to others to determine important character flaws like possessiveness and control. For example, when we are on the phone with a friend, girlfriend, or boyfriend, we should pretend that we need to get off the phone to talk to someone else. Pay attention to the person to see if they get agitated. We must learn to say no even when we could say yes to ensure that friendship or partnership can accept our NO. Friendships and love should be freeing, not restrictive, overbearing, or monopolizing all of your time or attention.

My Worthy
India Huntley

   (Themes: Betrayal, Domestic Violence, Physical Abuse & Drug Use)

I'm worthy of being alive. I'm smart, beautiful, and continuing to be independent. I don't need a man to make me happy. That's something that I had to learn and manage. I deserve to be happy with or without a man. I want to stand on my own two feet, to be strong. I'm a mother of two who wants to be better: better myself. Went through three different DV's with three different relationships. I could have died. But thank God, I prayed and now I'm still alive.

You betrayed me. As a man, you put your hands on me and continued to verbally abuse me. I'm worth a lot. I will become something. You told me I wouldn't be nothing, but God knows I'm worthy of being alive. I felt so torn. There were times I felt sore. I thought we would last forever, but you've shown me differently. Always accusing me and bringing up the past mistakes I've made. You betrayed me. It made me feel very upset, angry, and discouraged about our relationship. Doing drugs isn't me, but my choices were all on me. I forgive you, but I'll never forget the things you've done to me.

Commentary "My Worthy"

What do you feel you are worth? What are you good at, or what would someone say you are good for? Physical punches or powerful verbal blows to your self-esteem have a way of causing you to forget your worth. It causes you to ask yourself questions like, "Do I deserve this?" …"Why is this happening to me? … "What is wrong with me?" No one ever deserves to be abused. More importantly, domestic violence does not discriminate. It happens in all races, social-economic classes, and within all educational levels. If you have gone through this in the past, continue to tell yourself you are worthy.

Me
By Darvin Dowl

(Themes: Drug Use, Homelessness, and Recovery)

I am Me
Seen too much violence at an early age.
I am Me
Once was homeless,
scared every day of these ugly streets
I am Me
Started doing drugs to hide and forget the pain
I am Me
All alone, lost and confused
I am Me
Found help in drug recovery
I am Me
Feeling the sun on my face
I am Me
Seeing hope now, instead of despair
I am Me
Seeing the light at the end of the tunnel
That's Me
Who are You?

Commentary for "Me"

After you read this poem, make sure you read "I Am" By Peace. Both poets have a very similar message. They have faced homelessness. However, Darvin vividly explains an important source of trauma, community violence. Community violence such as fighting within your school or neighborhood, shooting deaths, and gang violence cause secondary trauma. Even when it doesn't seem like we are impacted by things within the community around us, it does impact our wellbeing greatly. Darvin explains seeing violence at an "early age" and refers to the "ugly streets" within his community. Take a moment to think about how you see the community where you live. Do you feel safe? Have you seen things happen in the past that are hard to forget?

The Chronic
By Cassandra Jenkins (aka Cassandra Is Free)
                              (Themes: Chronic Pain & Anxiety)

For the people who speculate
and tell me I don't look like what I'm going through
I'm supposed to say thank you
But sometimes pain makes it hard to speak
It's the chronic pain for me
Nights where I can't sleep, breathe,eat
Cause food always triggers it
Triggers more than people who tell me I don't look sick so I must be ok
They just don't see what it's doing to me
Because pain isn't always tangible
You can't hold it the way it holds you
It's not loosening its grip up
so there's days when I don't even wanna get up
Just wanna wrap myself in a blanket
Tell people what to do with their blanket statements
When they state that I should be happy, it's not worse
There are days when the only thing worse than the pain
would be not feeling anything
Times when it's so crippling
that the thought of my life ending doesn't sound all that bad
Waking up in agony
Headaches and body aches that linger like an unwanted houseguest
In my body, my body once my temple is now crucifying me daily
Until I've become a living sacrifice, feeling forsaken
So, when people tell me I don't look like what I'm going through, I cringe
because they act like you can't be both beautiful and broken
It's the chronic pain for me
Tired of explaining that invisible and imaginary aren't the same thing
Tired of explaining that there are good days and bad days
Days where I can run a marathon and days where I can't even run to my couch
I am not okay most days, because even on the days where it doesn't hurt,
my anxiety stays up to remind me that the pain is going to return

So, I wait for it, staring out the window like Celie looking for Mister

Cause' that pain is like a slap in the face,

so I'm waiting for signs that it's about to hit...

The effects don't exist to the naked eye

so outside looking in, I'm healthy

But if you could see how this pain turns me inside out,

you wouldn't mistake my cries for lies

Say I'm lazy on days I need to just rest

You're still in bed? Yes,

because sometimes it takes an extra hour, day, or week to get me started,

don't get me started

When I say the struggle is real, cause' it's a real struggle to exist

With this chronic illness

No cure, just ways to manage it

while trying to manage the damage it brings

But how do you manage when the only thing that helps chronic is chronic

Cause' my job is zero tolerance,

and if I lose it, I wouldn't have the bread for the bread n' butter anyway

So please don't tell me I don't look like what I'm going through

It feels more insinuation than compliment

More accuser than optimist

I wish I was Optimus, so I could transform people's way of thinking

and treating people with an invisible illness

Say it's supposed to make us stronger cause' it ain't kill us

What it does is weaken the spirit

and no this ain't a pity party

No, woah is me

Just wish some things were different

Like people not letting how someone looks decide if they believe their condition

So, for the people who speculate and tell me I don't look like what I'm going through...

Thank you

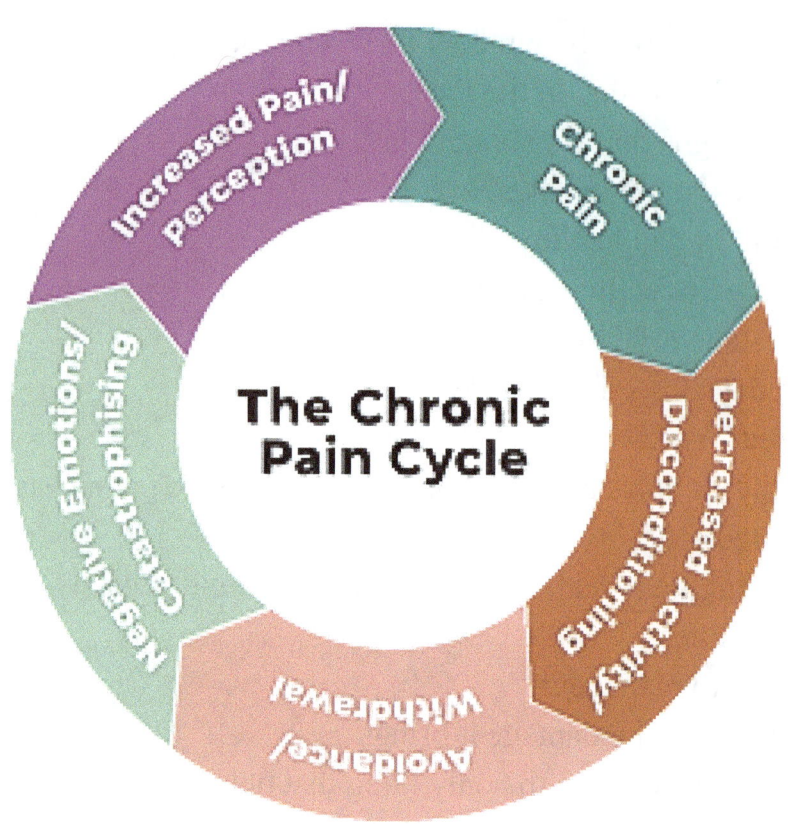

The Chronic Pain Cycle

(Increased Pain/Perception — Chronic Pain — Decreased Activity/Deconditioning — Avoidance/Withdrawal — Negative Emotions/Catastrophising)

Commentary for "The Chronic"

According to the Center for Disease Control (CDC), "In 2023, 24.3% of adults had chronic pain," but they are not the only age group dealing with it. Youth and teens also suffer chronic pain. Chronic pain can come from a variety of diseases and conditions. Also, it can come from unknown sources such as fibromyalgia. Those who suffer through this type of persistent pain spend countless hours at the doctor's office running tests, getting blood drawn, taking x-rays, (Magnetic Resonance Imaging) MRI's, and (Computed Tomography) CT scans. It can impact a person's ability to work, go to school, live on their own, or take care of themselves. Look at "The Chronic Pain Cycle" image and read each category. Could you imagine what your life would be like if you had to live with chronic pain?

Suicide or Homicide?
By Zeus Cruz

(Themes: Anxiety, Perseverance, and Determination)

Once, you were engulfed in a premonition of possession. Ambitious visions to overcome your fears and go beyond the limits of the stratosphere. Making inner demons turn apparitions. Yet, the lighthouse of your mind went dark and entered the state of decommission. Your hopes and dreams faded away due to unlawful living conditions. Similar to the inquisition where you stumbled and eventually crumbled to the opposition. A shell of yourself now. No longer familiar to your own recognition.

Shameful and pitiful to allow a mixed breed of an envious demonstrator. Mixed with a pompous, rambunctious hater to become your influencer. Enter into the chamber of your temple and be to your inner kingdom. The supreme ruler made a wager on their truth to become their consumer to now murdering the memories of your dreams. For they're the shooters, to become another soldier in their regime. For you fell to the spell of the recruiter.

You're slowly killing yourself as you gaze at the cut-out portraits made into a collage. An abstract view of a montage of how the real you was once there, and now it's a mirage. What you thought were allies were in fact enemies. The devil's entourage, who blended in perfectly with their camouflage, thought you would be given your flowers. Yet, it was a dead corsage. Sold your soul, only to be bought at a higher price. Arbitrage. The torture from them became the death of you. Your dreams were meant to be sabotaged.

But the reality is that their attempt of homicide is really your version of suicide. For you let doubt and anxiety enter your mind and reside. By design, allowed ego and conviction to collide and now the best part of you has died. Because in the end, you yourself have the power to control the outcome, and not let others or levels of uncertainty place upon you, dominion, to kill your moment of opportunity, and become their minion, or worse, their murder victim. To make you lose hold of your beliefs just, cause' of their opinions. Never let one murder your ambition. To your reckless abandon… Instead, die trying to make your dreams happen.

Definitions for "Suicide or Homicide"

premonitions= a strong feeling that something bad is about to happen

stratosphere = the layer of the earth below the troposphere which is the lower level of the earth's atmosphere

apparitions= a ghost or ghost-like image of a person

decommission= withdraw something, especially weapons or military from service

pompous= effectively or irritatingly grand or self- important

rambunctious= informal, uncontrollably filled with lively energy or excitement

regime= a government, especially an authoritarian one

montage= the process or technique of selecting, editing, and piecing together separate sections of film to form a continuous whole

mirage= an optical illusion caused by atmospheric conditions, especially the appearance of a sheet of water in a desert on a hot road caused by the refraction of light from the sky by heated air

entourage= a group of people attending or surrounding an important person

arbitrage= the practice of simultaneously buying and selling an asset in different markets to profit from price differences

sabotage= deliberately destroy, damage, or obstruct something, especially for political or military advantage

dominion= sovereignty or control

minion= a follower or underling of a powerful person, especially an unimportant one

Commentary for "Suicide or Homicide?"

I heard someone give this quote during a lecture, "Abandonment wounds aren't always about someone abandoning you… it's you abandoning yourself on the pathway to your dreams." This is self-sabotage. We can be our worst critics. We may tell ourselves things we would never tell anyone else. When you have a dream, fight hard to protect it. Fight even harder when the one who is trying to destroy it is you. Never allow your own insecurities to make you too scared to dream. Dreams don't take into account who you are right now. Dreams only see who you will be. Allow yourself to dream. Believe the dream will become a reality.

Hate When I Tell the Truth
By Zeus Cruz

(Themes: Toxic Relationships & Mental Abuse)

I can't believe your method of intoxication, of infatuation, would eventually be my nonfiction, should have stood firm to my predisposition, my Spidey sense tingling intuition, and not succumb to the stipulations, to know you was not good for me, poisonous, a hologram of a vixen, with your spells and elixirs, anything regarding us, I had to ask for permission, you became a drug to me, like prescriptions, which you happily fed into the addiction, cause' you wanted control, through dependency, like a God through religion, the word toxic was more than a word to describe you, you're the actual definition, wishing I could go back in time, a multiverse of a rewind, and undo the decision, of being intertwined, with a conniving slithering serpentine, turn me lunatic, so, to keep a straight jacket around my mind, I'd rather die alone to suicide, then to continue to be by your side, doesn't matter anymore, for you are guilty of homicide, for I'm already dead inside, only one question remains, why can't I say goodbye

I try to understand why, only to become more manic, of how easily you stretch the truth, as if honesty was elastic, how your version of peace, is to create more havoc, to bring more darkness, to the abyss of madness, burn a rabbit hole, into my heart, like your words were laced with acid, visceral is the visuals, a combatant so graphic, you once took my breath away, asthmatic, to now being alien to me, interstellar to destructive galactic, you're so insanely toxic, to be honest, and you kept your promise, saying you would be the death of me, plaguing me with your sickness, robbing me of my antibiotics, screaming at me, of the voices in your subconscious, pleading for you to disregard your conscience

It's a cat and mouse game, and I fell for the trap, voodoo conjuring with your witchcraft, use me up and throw away my love like riff raff, one plus one equals the two of us, but you never cared much for math, my soul slowly dying, the word sucker written on my epitaph, but no longer, for your possession, turned into my resurrection, your manipulative powers, cut in half, the person you took for granted, has taken your blessings away, and now you wave forfeit upon the Flagstaff, no point to go on the warpath, for you to feel my wrath, I rather let karma get you, and I'll have the last laugh

Definitions for "Hate When I Tell the Truth"

infatuation =   an intense, but short-lived passion or admiration for someone or something

predisposition= a liability or tendency to hold a particular attitude or act in a particular way

intuition=   the ability to understand something immediately, without the need for conscious reasoning

succumb=   failed to resist pressure, temptation, or some negative force

stipulations=   a condition that is specified as part of an agreement

elixirs=   a magical or medicinal potion

conniving=   given to or involved in conspiring to do something immoral, illegal, or harmful

havoc=   widespread destruction

visceral=   relating to the viscera or the internal organs in the main cavities of the body, especially in the abdomen. i.e the intestines

interstellar=   occurring or situated between stars

galactic=   relating to a galaxy or galaxies

epitaph=   a short inscription often on a tombstone or monument honoring a deceased person

manipulative=   characterized by a person having no morals or principles, a person who is not honest or fair

forfeit=   lose or be deprived of property or a right or privilege as a penalty for wrongdoing

flagstaff=   another term for flagpole.

Commentary for "Hate When I Tell the Truth"

The "Types of Toxic People" chart shows many characteristics and categories of toxic people. Toxic people pollute your judgement, poison your spirit, and overcome you with their venom.

Activity for "Hate When I Tell the Truth"

Choose the type of toxic person from the lines in the poem that best fits the chart.

1."I had to ask for permission"

_____

2. "turn me lunatic, so, to keep a straight jacket around my mind"

_____

3. "which you happily fed into the addiction, cause' you wanted control, through dependency"

_____

types of toxic people

THE NARCISSIST

only cares about themselves

lacks empathy

truly believes they are better than
everyone around them

THE CONTROLLER

tries to control everything
around them
needs to be in charge of every decision
makes you feel like
you can't do anything right

THE DRAMA MAGNET

feeds off of gossip and drama

drama seems to "follow them"
(they create it)

puts you in
uncomfortable positions

THE ENERGY VAMPIRE

drains you of energy, overwhelms you

creates problems and feeds on the
negativity

criticizes and bullies
you

THE COMPULSIVE LIAR

tells white lies
constantly
manipulates and gaslights you
master of guilt trips

THE GREEN EYED

cannot be happy for
other people's good fortune

plays the victim

minimizes other people to feel
better about themselves

Two-Weeks Notice
By Kesha Cole

(Themes: Domestic Violence & Physical Abuse)

I turned in my two-weeks notice today
I'm so glad no one noticed
How bad I was feeling this day
No one asked me if I was ok,
when I turned in my two-weeks notice today,
Because I do a good job of hiding it,
No one knows when I wake up crying
Deep down inside it feels like I'm dying
So, I pretend that I'm taking a vacation
to get out of this bad situation
But my spirit is losing its patience
When I turned in my two-weeks notice today,
he knew something was up
but he couldn't put his finger on it
Meanwhile, I'm just trying not to get hit,
as I prepare to leave
It's a nightmare
Things start to disappear
First my birth certificate,
then my social security card
The other day, he hit me really hard
I was so out of it all I could do was sob
No more trying to compromise
No more crying all night
No more getting jumped on before work
No more trying to hide my hurt.
So, as I turned in my two-weeks notice today
I pray, there has to be another way.

Commentary for "Two-Weeks Notice"

At first glance, you may think this poem is about putting in a two-week notice to leave a job. You see the author losing her patience and pretending to be on vacation. As you look further, you realize this is about leaving a toxic relationship, not a job. However, ACTUALLY giving a person two-weeks notice, or notice at all for that matter is very dangerous and can cost you your life. A good plan to escape is to ensure the person is at work, or definitely away from home for an extended timeframe. Have the police come to stand guard until you move your belongings. Talk to police about filing any necessary protection orders.

The Ohio Domestic Violence Network (ODVN) and Women Helping Women assistance programs can help you with relocation services. They can provide you with a safe place, normally a hotel or safe house to live in. Depending on funding, other services can be provided including rental assistance, utility payments, and other necessities to help until you are securely living alone.

BLIP
By J. Summers

(Themes: Colorism & Discrimination)

So, the other day, me and my friend were having a conversation, and she described herself as a BLIP: Black Live In Person. I told her that is one of the nicest statements I've ever heard... I've been called many things in my life and this one is the one that describes me the best. We looked up the definition and it provided even more reason for me to use this description for myself. It read...
" an unexpected, minor, and typically temporary deviation from a general trend. "
That definition describes me more than anything else I've been called in my life. I've been BLACK, MELANATED, a BIPOC, AFRICAN-AMERICAN, NEGRO, SUNKISSED, EBONY, A MINORITY, BROWN, COLORED, called an ISRAELITE, TOKEN, a few N words I will not repeat, and a few phrases when none of those descriptions fit me. You're not like the rest of them. You're a good one. But you seem so educated. What side of town did you grow up on? Hey Chief, hey Big Guy, and the one that always gets on my nerves... What race are you?
In my life, I've never let the color of my skin, my melanation, or ancestry dictate what I can do, because I was told from childhood that I can be anything, and that's exactly what I decided to do. I'm an artist, author, publisher, poet, event coordinator, City Official, actor, bridge builder, mentor, father, here to listen, shoulder to lean on, cry if you need to, fist for defense, and I will walk through any door my purpose leads me to. I was always told if you change for those around you, you will eventually lose you. So, I go to everything with a smile on my face just as I am, because I know someone needs to see the person that looks like you. Someone needs to know that these parts of life are not off limits, because of the color of your hue. So, I embrace being a BLIP, because although my time might be finite, I am definitely someone that does not stand by the status quo. I know that interruption is the normal way that things go. Bringing a lot of people together into places they did not know they could go. So, wherever you go, embrace the deviation of not looking like everyone else and inspiring someone to do something new.

Definitions of "BLIP"

BLIP =	made up acronym for Black Live In Person
melanation=	a term that refers to the process by which melanin, a pigment responsibility for the color of the skin, hair, and eyes is produced and distributed within the human body
status quo=	the existing state of affairs, especially regarding social or political issues
deviation=	the action of departing from the action or from an established course or accepted standard

Commentary for "BLIP"

Discrimination takes many forms. Colorism is one of those forms. The Oxford Language Dictionary defines colorism as "prejudice or discrimination against individuals with a dark skin tone, typically among people of the same ethnic or racial groups." In the Latinx community this is called pigmentocracy. Do you know that many darker skinned people are paid less than their lighter skin peers? Sometimes, those who are dark-skinned are viewed as less educated, less attractive, more confrontational and angry, and more likely to be involved in criminal activity.

Cattails
By Zeus Cruz

(Themes: Isolation & Redemption)

My spirit aches with torment
As I journey through this **bog** of deceit
As my footprints lead to the unknown
A trail made that I wish no one would follow
Feel as if I am now baptized
As I'm splashed with the water of truth
I used to cleanse myself of the mud stains
That signifies my past mistakes
The swamp of memories
Now resembles a confession booth
As the dirt of my transgressions
Offset my reflection
For I do not recognize myself anymore
I find comfort hiding behind the **cattails**
So, no one can acknowledge my presence
For I am ashamed of what I have become

I only show glimpses of myself
In between the spaces
As the cattails sway from the harsh breeze
And yet, delight and bewilderment
Becomes etched across my face
As I discover a trace of steps
Just to the side of me
And I realize I am not alone
In this trek of redemption
The air was foul
And now has a pleasant aroma of hope
Once numb to my senses
I now feel the warmth of vindication
The sunlight is piercing through
The droplets laying upon the cattails
Creating miniature prisms of life
Back into my soul
And as I walk out from behind
What I deemed as a barricade
Amazement came within my view
And brought tears to my eyes
As I saw my loved ones run towards me
To embrace me
And this is the moment I knew
There is such a thing
As a second chance

Definitions for "Cattails"

bog=   wet, muddy ground too soft to support a heavy body
cattails=   a tall, reedlike marsh plant with a brown, velvety, cylindrical
               head of numerous tiny flowers (see picture)
bewilderment= a feeling of confusion
vindication=   the action of clearing someone of blame or suspicion
barricade=   a barrier put up across a path to prevent movement of opposing
               forces

Commentary of "Cattails"

Being disconnected from family and friends for any reason can be painful. The author's metaphor takes him into a swampy area hidden behind the cattails. We may see ourselves hidden behind the walls we put up but ask yourself are the walls keeping you safe or putting you in danger of isolation. Isolation is very different from just having time alone. Having time alone allows you to see yourself and work on yourself. Isolation puts you behind a barricade where only loneliness and sadness are there present with you.

Two Minutes of Your Time
By J. Summers

(Themes: Empowerment & Encouragement)

Good morning, good afternoon, good evening and good night. Wherever you might be in the world I appreciate you for reading. To whoever might be reading this or listening to this it's going to be okay. I may not know you or even get a chance to meet you in this lifetime, but some part of me is present with you at this moment and I want to say, it's going to be okay. Life is hard and we all have our difficulties to face. But as long as you're still willing to get back up, you can find better ways to accomplish your goals and investigate why you failed. Do not try again and get the same results. It's going to be okay. I don't know what part of life this might have reached you at, but I can tell you even if I am no longer here to recite these words, it's going to be okay. Give yourself time and take a deep breath. Have you done it? Okay, now think about all the things in life that you had to face before this moment... Did you survive them? Are you present now to make a decision that will better your life? So, I believe you will survive whatever is troubling you at this moment and it's going to be okay. There's one small favor I have to ask if you are reading this or hearing this... Give yourself a hug, in this moment, because the next might be too late. I want you to tell yourself I love you and thank you for all the mistakes we've made along our journey, because they are ours to own and they make us the most unique individuals that creation has inspired. It's okay if you look weird to the person next to you who may not know why you're loving on yourself so hard. Healing is a process and it's okay if it takes a lifetime, because it's the only way you'll get to know yourself. I hope this moment helped and if there's someone still staring at you strangely, you're more than welcome to pass this message along... It's going to be okay. I may not be here for your darkest moments or greatest joys, but in this moment, we have eternity.

Thank you for reading,
I hope you have a better morning, afternoon, evening and night.

Commentary for "Two Minutes of Your Time"

This poem not only empowers us and encourages us, it also asks us to, "Give yourself time and take a deep breath." How we breathe is a direct reflection of what we are going through. When we are overwhelmed and stressed, we tend to breathe using quick, shallow breaths, that leave our chest barely expanding. If serious physical activities like running, boxing, and exercising require that you learn to breathe, what do you expect is needed to face obstacles, deal with family, go to work and school, and continue to move forward in our lives? Breathe In. Release. Breathe In again. Release Again. It truly is going to be okay.

Yes, I Have Trust Issues, Somewhere in the Middle
By J Summers

(Theme: Betrayal)

If you're reading this or listening to this, you already know why we came here...
Yes, I have trust issues, but I learned them somewhere along the middle. If you
take offense to this and somehow think that I'm attacking you, you might want to
look in the mirror, because we all believe the lie about something or someone at
some point in time. I'm just using mine to get what's off my mind. See, I have trust
issues, because every time I think something's going right there's always that little
reminder in the back of my mind that this could go completely wrong. Somehow, I
wasted my time on someone or something that I found precious. But in the end, it
turned out to be a lesson of just not getting it right this time. See, I have trust
issues, because every time I tried to give someone or something this ocean of
experience, I've learned through trial and error they were really just looking for a
bottle of water. Maybe to dip their toe in to see if there really was depth here. I
have trust issues, because the sky is not actually blue, and growing up my entire
childhood I was told there were 9 planets. By the time I hit adulthood, there were
only eight to view. I have trust issues, because every single fairy tale, folklore,
childhood bedtime story growing up never came true... Except for the trauma part
of losing a parent or two, going through difficult times, stress, trials and
tribulations and finally figuring out that it might not have been you. I have trust
issues. I grew up hearing about racism, prejudice, and crooked politicians. I found
most of those people are just like me and you. They never actually got to meet the
opposition. They just lived on the fairytale of this is what that statistical person is
like from the outside view. I have trust issues and somewhere in the middle of
growing up and finding my purpose, I found out... Most issues start with you.
Trusting too many things. That someone or something is wrong if they don't think
like you, when really the first person you're supposed to be able to trust is you. I
have trust issues, because I know somewhere in the middle of me reciting this, or
you reading this, you might have blanked out for a moment or two. That part that I
stuck in the middle was really important, but it got glazed over cuz' this might
have been too long for you.

Definitions for "Yes, I Have Trust Issues, Somewhere in the Middle"

opposition= resistance or dissent expressed in action or argument

statistical=   relating to the use of collecting, organizing, and preserving data

Commentary for "Yes, I Have Trust Issues, Somewhere in the Middle"

Think of all the ways we fail to trust ourselves: overthinking, being unsure of our choices even when they are good ones and focusing on negative things. Look at the image by Summit Malibu. It's ok to have these feelings every now and then, but if they begin to take over your life, ask yourself if you could be experiencing rumination.

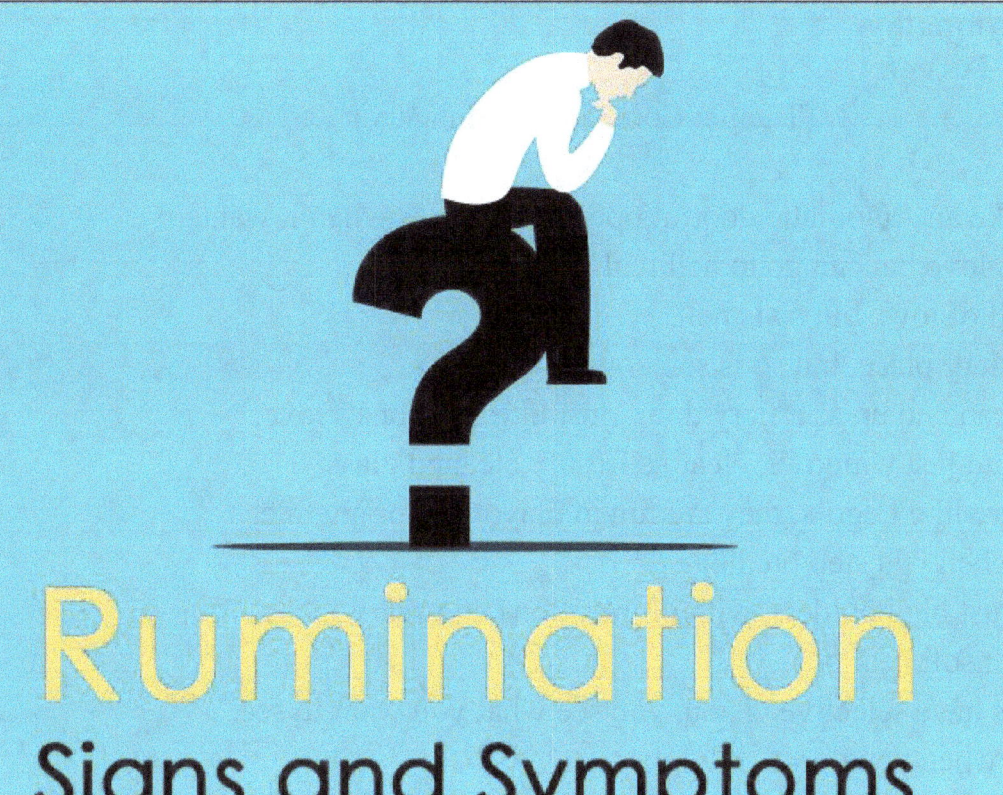

Rumination
Signs and Symptoms

- Persistent negative thinking
- Overthinking about the past or future
- Depression or anxiety
- Mood swings and irritability
- Withdrawing from family and friends
- Fatigue or sleep issues
- Trouble focusing and concentrating
- Feeling sad or hopeless
- Low self-esteem

Love is Sympathy
By Lexie Turner

(Theme: Comparative Imagery)

Love is like an Automatic door; it opens and closes when it wants
Heaven is love but can go to hell real quick.
Life is full of love, but so is hell.
Hell is a fiery place, but so is someone's heart,
violence can end up as a fiery thing, just like someone's love.
Humans are just windows, clear as freshly cleaned glass.
Women are like Lego's, they are fun to play with for a while,
but hurt when you step on them.
Men are just big boulders, with ill intentions and scary faces.
Some with soft hearts.
Your eyes have selective vision, you see what you want to see,
and don't when you don't.
Violence is like an overused drug with a lasting effect,
you take it and then regret it later.
Drugs can be used for bad things, or good things. Love is a drug.
Death causes things to vanish, just like ashes of a person, love vanishes.
My Love is sympathy, but my sympathy will soon turn into anger.

Commentary for "Love is Sympathy"

This young author speaks with proverbial wisdom that is beyond her years.
Have you ever heard of the saying, "It's a thin line between love and hate?" This
author says, "Love is like an Automatic door, it opens and closes when it wants.
Have you ever had someone betray you and then think back on how you really saw
straight through them? Lexie Turner says, "Humans are just windows, clear as
freshly cleaned glass." Have you been taught that every action has a consequence?
She says, "Violence is like an overused drug with a lasting effect, you take it and
then regret it later. Circle your favorite lines in this poem.

They Don't Deserve It Pt. 1
By Louis Barnes

(Theme: Domestic Violence)

What's up world? There is something we need to discuss.

It doesn't just affect me; it affects all of us.

Why do so many women have to be abused by their significant other?

Why do so many women die due to the hands of their lover?

Tell me why you belittle her, threaten her and put her down?

Come home drunk, bad day at work and knock her to the ground.

So, you the "man," because you ball your fist up and black her eye?

What, you get a kick out of seeing her scared, shaking as you make her cry?

If she talks back to you, you punch her in her mouth, bust, and swell her lip.

I guess beating your woman makes you cool. I'm telling you, it ain't hip.

If y'all don't know by now, I'm talking about domestic violence.

See, it's serious. Time to talk about it and stop moving in silence.

Shouldn't no woman have a partner that makes her fear for her life.

Why would you put a gun to her head, or come at her with a knife?

Approximately 51,100 women die due to their man.

One woman is killed every ten minutes, time to take a stand.

I'm writing this, because it's time to spread the word.

On this subject, I'm trying to reach someone and be heard.

Now to you so called big men, but cowards is what I call you.

You quick to hit a woman. When a man steps to you, what do you do?

Drop your head, turn, walk away, and tuck your tail.

Guys like you are sickening. You deserve to burn in hell.

Tell me what you get out of causing pain with all that abuse.

See hitting your woman, you don't win. In the end, you actually lose.

You think it's cool having your woman live in fear.

You're supposed to be her protector, but she feels fear when you come near.

Ladies, when he hits you, it's not your fault. You're not to blame.

You don't need a man to disrespect you or call you out of your name.

You're more than someone to beat on. You're not his punching bag.

Y'all are special and precious. Not to be treated like an old dirty rag.

Commentary for "They Don't Deserve It"

Instead of a commentary, please let's take a moment of silence for every life that has been lost.

Pain
By Trenton Duttenhoffer

(Theme: Chronic Pain)

Pain. Like a web, it is so interconnected within our bodies.
For some, pain is easy to escape.
While for others, much like a web, once you're caught you can't get out. Pain.
You are the prey to the spider. Pain.
It comes in an endless number of forms. Pain.
You can not escape it like the cycle of life. Pain.
We run endlessly around it to try to understand. Pain.
While you may not be able to find the end of it,
you can find the beginning of it. Pain.
To escape the endless web, you must accept it. Pain.
You must accept the darkness of the pain to help understand why it exists.
For pain is what moves us; it's what makes us wish to thrive, survive, to live.
To truly live, you must accept the pain.
For Pain is what makes us move forward. Pain is nature.
Pain.

Commentary for "Pain"

We are all on varied levels of our healing journeys. This poem may be hard for some to hear, but it is another way to look at pain. Compare this poem to Cassandra Is Free's poem, "The Chronic." For those who navigate through life in chronic pain, it seems to follow the grief cycle: denial, anger, bargaining, depression, and acceptance. Not necessarily in that order, and it definitely does not mean that once you made it through all five, you are finished. Experiencing physical pain is traumatic. Be careful how you treat others around you who may be suffering in silence.

Just As I Had Started
By Trenton Duttenhoffer

(Theme: Anxiety & Encouragement)

(A Poem for Educators)

I stepped into my classroom, all full of joy,

Curious about my new students— and our recess toys.

I was eager and ready, preparing away,

Like lightning, it struck… the first day.

However, could it be?

Thirty-four eyes all looking at me,

I was the one they'd look up to, trustingly.

Five days a week, ten months of the year,

Sometimes painful to look in the mirror.

As I grew closer to each precious child,

Noticed the glimmer, the spark, the wild.

The pure of heart and innocence,

Praying their hearts feels less dense.

An escape so safe,

Oh look…there goes the date.

Love and laughter began to bloom,

Filling our little but growing classroom.

Weeks become months, and every day,

Each child taught me more than words can say.

The lessons I've taught and continue to teach,

Little is greater than what they've taught me.

Patience is a virtue, some may say,

To be at peace in the midst of day.

A deep breath, a hug, a mere cat drawing,

Who knew my anxieties would go crawling?

To notice and wonder the lives of each one,

Is to recognize that I am not done.

The mission has started, and I will stay,

To grasp the new truth of each and every day.

Love boldly the unique and tender-hearted,

Showing up and giving it my all,

Just as I had started.

Commentary for "Just as I Started"

Although this is a publication for students, we included this to ensure we encourage all of our educators. Teaching is one of the most underpaid professions. You are the reason they keep coming back to teach hoping something they do or say will positively impact your life.

Activity for "Just as I Started"

Write and deliver a quick, handwritten letter to three teachers. Tell each teacher at least one way they have made a difference in your life.

The Survivors (Dedication to Bob Marley)
By SoL (aka Mista STAYonLit)
(Themes: Freedom, Survival, & Perseverance)

Tell Me Where's A Survivor,
Black Survivor
I'm Looking for The Survivors,
The Black Survivors
Oh, I Found A Survivor
Yes, A Black Survivor
I'm The Survivor,
Black Survivor

On an episode of "Like It Is" with the late great, Gil Noble, which you can view on YouTube, Father Marley was asked what led to the writing of his most militant effort of a record known as "Survival". His answer was the 1976 shooting which injured Marley, his wife, and his manager. Due to no fatalities from the event, he **surmised** that it was indeed Survival. Afterwards, Gil proceeded to ask, "What happened on the night he was shot?" It is here in this piece I offer my interpretation of his words in response:

It was about 3 nights before that ambush in the night,
hit my door on Hope Road…gunfire bombarded me in a dream.
Bullets ran through my arms, torso and chest left red as I turned to see my own mother caught one to the head.
Naturally, any man would adhere to fear.
Being that death feeling so near, so close as here.

142

That's when I hear "Don't Run. Stand Up."
"Despite what is happening, I repeat this to you now: Don't Run. Stand Up."
So, when the gunmen came in 3 days to do what gunmen do,
I recalled that visual proof to be my ultimate truth.
Don't Run. Stand Up. I Choose to Stay Alive; I Am Determined to Survive.

'Cause I'm A Survivor,
A Black Survivor
Just Like You're A Survivor,
'Nother Black Survivor
Fore We Are Survivors,
Yes, Them Black Survivors
We Are Survivors,
The Black Survivors

Survivors, Black Survivors
21st Century Natural Born Freedom Fighters
Legendary, **Luminary,** African Souls on Fire
Lit by The Sun, Spirits Ever Young, Gold in Our Blood,
the Iron Lion Pride of Zion
Loc'd Eyez on Forward Movement, Though We Never Forget
Where We Came From
Marching Through The Wintry Cold Winds of America
Where Their Aim is to Dismay, Maim, Frame, and Slay Us like The Buffalo
But Souljahs Multiply Not Die, 'Cause High or Low We Are Beautifully Bold,
Adaptively Adequate, Intimately Innovative,
Relentlessly Resilient, Spiritually Sophisticated,
Compassion, Vigilant; Bravery, Militant;
Potential, Limitless; Any Thought of Killing It? Finish It!
Or Keep On Underestimating Our Innerstanding of the Situation
For Each One of Us Has The Tools of Creation
With Hands Made Strong by The Hands of The Almighty
To Hold On Through The Troubles and Struggles Day'ly & Night'ly
In Spite of The Tears That River Our Face

Despite The Fears That Slither Our Way
Our Hearts Beat On With That One Drop Rhythm
Staying The Course On Hope's Road Past The Babylonian System
Still Waking Up to Live, Turning Over Every Stone
Till They Wake Up to See Us Turn't Into Cornerstones
We Are Not Conquered, We Are The Independence of Zimbabwe
We Are The Liberators, and Revolution is Coming at Our Pace
So, Ride Natty Ride, in The City of Cin Cin, Shine Nati Shine
And If They Come to Ambush in The Night,
Remember This Good Word to Recite
"Don't Run, Stand Up"; Your Life is Your Right, Your Right is To Live
So, Get Up, Stand Up, Fight On…And Live!

"We're The Survivors,
The Black Survivors
We're The Survivors,
The Black Survivors
We're The Survivors,
Yes, The Black Survivors
We Are Survivors,
Black Survivors"

Lyrics were Composed in SoL
Hook Interpolates the Chorus from Survival by Bob Marley & The Wailers
Inspired by Bob Marley Interview w/ Gil Noble - "Like It Is" in NYC [1980]

Definitions for "The Survivors (Dedication to Bob Marley)"

surmised= suppose that something is true without having evidence to confirm it

luminary= a person who inspires or influences others, especially one prominent in a particular sphere

Commentary for "The Survivors (Dedication to Bob Marley)"

Bob Marley, a social justice activist, songwriter, and performer was a luminary. He introduced the world to Reggae music. His songs included themes of peace, unity, and love. Now that you have read and listened to this tribute by SoL (aka Mista STAYonLit), please look up Bob Marley's YouTube video, "Get Up Stand Up."

I Have Become Echo
An old man speaks to his son
By Mike Olson

(Themes: Caregiving, Alzheimer's, & Dementia)

My son,   I know
You can see my body wandering from me
There's nothing you can do
Please   try to understand
I am not abandoning you
Please   be patient if I repeat myself   from time
to time the same words may ricochet out of me

I am becoming echo.

Remember when I read the same story to you every night
until you fell asleep   it's like that
it's just me   telling stories to myself
until I tumble asleep
it's me   just grabbing at memories as they fly away
like dollar bills in the vortex money cage.
I need to grab all I can

before I become echo.

Please   be patient   I may repeat myself
I may forget to bathe   don't worry
It's just not that important anymore
I'm not pushing you away
There's no one left I need to impress
It's not me letting myself go
It's me letting myself be

Remember when you were small –
how you hated bath time
because there were too many games left to play
because there was no time left to play them?
same here and   by the way   did I mention
I sometimes tell stories to myself?
Please   try to understand

I am becoming echo

If I am slow   if I fall behind
if you can't take me to the zoo with my grandchildren
your children
Please give me your hand   stroll with me
Like I strolled with you   hold me
like I held you when   you   could not walk
Don't be sad   I'm not abandoning you

When that time comes,   *I am not abandoning you*
Oh, did I mention   I may forget to bathe?

Please   don't look at me that way
when I scroll the wrong way, text with full words or none at all,
look for dials and clickers instead buttons and gizmos.
Remember   when I showed you how to use a spoon, remember
the long strokes of brush and comb, the ointments, the powders
that kept you safe and wonderous in your feebleness
Please   try to understand
I don't want to become echo.

If I forget what I have named you if I forget the terrain of your face
If a minute into our conversation I forget what we're talking about
Please   don't be angry with me
Please   help me stay on my road
Remember   how I taught you the ABCs
Remember   how I taught you Dosey-Doe and Doe-Ray-Me

146

Remember the day when you finally could say   *Daddy*
I didn't need the word
I always knew you recognized me from your smile
Please know   I just want that same moment
if for only a moment
however trite that may sound
Hey,   did I mention   please be careful
memories may ricochet out of me
I have become echo.

Definitions for "I Have Become Echo"

ricochet=   of a bullet, shell, or other projectile rebound one or more times off of
             a surface

vortex=   a mass of whirling fluid or air, especially a whirlpool or whirlwind

Commentary for "I Have Become Echo"

One of the hardest times of my life was the eight months my grandmother spent being in home hospice care with my mother and I. She suffered Alzheimer's, a type of dementia, and end-stage lung disease. I remember one day in particular that was hard for me. She noticed I was crying. Although she had no way of knowing why, she told me she knew something was wrong if I was crying. She was convinced. It was so hard to see a person who had stayed clean all my life to refuse to shower, because she thought she had showered the day, even minutes before. The memory loss seemed to have no rhyme or reason. She would forget those closest to her and remember those who wouldn't even take the time to call or come for a visit. There were so many days I sat in silence just waiting for our normal conversation to return even if she'd echo something she had already spoken. For information on Alzheimer's and Dementia visit https://www.alz.org .

While Summer Left…
By Mike Olson

(Theme: Grief & Death)

That summer when I came to visit her
I saw another woman in my mother's skin.
She was seated in her favorite chair,
face glistening from Arizona sweat.

Few words visited that day.
Her old self, finally visible,
sat with me watching her favorite shows,
laughing as she usually would –

no mention of the other woman,
no mention of her missing breasts,
no mention of her scars hidden
beneath her silencing scarves.

I was comfortable disappearing with her
while summer strolled away from us.
We watched what fall leaves there were
elope with old familiar winds –

what was left of their lives not captured,
never scraped into caretaker bags to be
hauled away, cremated, forgotten.
They had lived, left how they wanted.
Then winter came.

Commentary for "While Summer Left…"

When you have loved ones who are going through sickness and pain, one of the hardest parts is watching their physical appearance deteriorate from things like weight loss, swollenness and weight gain, mobility issues, changes to their skin, hair, and countless other things that can change rapidly. Although caregivers often feel alone and resentful of those in the family who do not help with caregiving, those who are away, living out of town, or just unable to watch their decline may deal with a tremendous amount of pain and grief as well.

A Letter to My Depression
By Brianna Chenault

(Theme: Depression)

To my depression-
You dirty bum. I hate you and everything you stood for.

That's it.
I ain't got too much more to say to you
After all, you decided to try and
take my last breath before God did

You are the reason why I thought it better to die than live
trapped inside the prison created by my mind
You the reason my mind was a prison in the first place
My spirit, the new snitch on the block
Running trying to tell God what my thoughts did
Thinking that would help get freedom
Not knowing what that really cost
My spirit became battered and bruised because of you
But I'm not telling you nothing new
You knew all that didn't you
Figured you'd found yourself a victim in me
so you pounced and sunk your teeth in deep
Before I knew it you pimped me out to the public
Using my insecurities to weaken me
Had me servicing everyone else's needs, but my own
Made me believe I couldn't survive you, but I also couldn't survive without you

My life no longer a good enough reason to live
You forced other people to be my "why"
I had surrendered to rotting away on the inside
Time no longer mattered, because the moment you sentenced me to life
Mine was over

Now I'm labeled a statistic
Everybody prejudging me, because of the time I did
People treating me differently once they found out where I'd been
Everyone calling me crazy when I tell them I turned myself in
to avoid doing a long bid
Little do they know,
Outpatient felt just like probation

I may never live a normal life now
All because of you
Depression, you were more than my prison system -you were the warden too
Creating your own made-up rules
Forcing me into submission even though you already held all the power
You were always right there to punish me if I ever felt too happy
If I ever enjoyed life too much
If I ever decided life was actually worth living you made sure I regretted it

You had my mind more corrupt than the US government
Your enforcers target people who look like me
Your affiliates love attacking minorities
At alarming; yet, underreported rates
Least likely to be helped let alone believed
But first to be victimized
Look how many black boys can't get you out their minds
Got them convinced this is the normal way of life
Dealing with you ain't nothing and real ones all gotta' do it sometime

So again, screw you and everything you stand for
You dirty, raggedy liar
You had me believing my appeals for help would never work
That there was no use in trying to live a life outside of you
That I couldn't hold down a job without them finding out about you
You twisted my thoughts into thinking life wasn't worth living
When the truth is, my time spent inside with you was the only time I'll spend dying
Now I spend all my freedom outside thriving

Honestly, this poem is running on because my sentence may not have an end
Those who know-know I may have to serve again
Escaping you may have been a bit felonious in your eyes
But it meant getting my life back
I gave you more than a fair share of my time
You may have got me caught up in your pipeline
but remember you're the repeat offender
I've liberated myself from you before and I can do it again
Never forget, I will always win

Commentary for "A Letter to My Depression"
Mental illness is a repeat offender. Someone who is suffering gets the help they need through therapy and/or medications. Then as soon as they start feeling better, some people stop taking the necessary medication and relapse into a mental health setback. This yo-yo effect of being back and forth, off and on medications, seems to send them spiraling down even further. The National Alliance of Mental Health states 1 in 20 adults have serious mental illness. For youth ages 13-18, 1 out of 5 suffer as well. If you are suffering, please call the PIRC, juvenile psychiatric center, at 513-636-4124.

Dedication to My Baby Girl
By Brianna Chenault

(Theme: Rape & Empowerment)

(My parents were always overprotective, because they didn't want me to be a statistic. According to the Center for Disease Control, (CDC), 1 in 4 women experience completed or attempted rape. 1 in 4 girls experience child sexual abuse.)

There are 12 women in 2 generations of my bloodline on one side
Regardless of when I was added into the equation
The odds were never in my favor
This math only makes me another statistic
Except in my family, it ain't 1 in every 4
It be more like everyone hiding their truth behind closed doors
Hiding their tears behind a smile that's actually yours
Pretending like it never happened since no one knew how to deal with it
So, no one ever dealt with it, they just pretend it never happened
Even after you told someone that it happened
I guess that's how we all got so good at acting

I remember when I started acting
I don't remember how old I was
I just know it was before I turned 13
I guess me repressing that memory didn't stop me from getting PTSD
But what can you say for prominent trauma
spawning deep from secrets under covers
Perpetually trapped stressed due to this repressed memory
Psychological tendons suppressing delicate stories
That was the first time I remember learning my "no"
could mean absolutely nothing
And all I ever told my parents was that my "no" meant nothing
How could I be honest and tell them our family members were thieves
And what they stole was a part of me

So, I just told them what happened under the covers
But we all know the real nightmares hide under the bed
Behind closed doors
Around corners the family refuses to look
If they really knew how much was took, would it have made a difference?
Wasn't it family tradition to ignore the predators in the bloodline?
Instead of eliminating them, we excused them so there continued to be a next time
Didn't we just accept their excuses,
and force Baby Girl to bear the burden of their brutal behavior?

Had me asking myself questions like:
What good would it do to tell the full truth
when I wasn't the first one it happened to?
Why create more chaos when it was just my turn to experience the family curse?
Could comfort have cast it out, the spell of me thinking it was my fault?
Why not become a creature of habit and just be quiet about what happened?
Especially, when I was expected to explain what I couldn't fully comprehend
I was only a child, how could I actually understand?
Yet, the responsibility of accountability got put on my shoulders
Like I was supposed to know what to do
Like it was my job to make him tell the truth
Being forced to confront the person who stole the innocence from you
before you grieved its loss, wasn't the help I needed

At the time, I saw my power trapped behind their eyes every time I closed mine
Body still violated though the violation wasn't violent
Just silent and coerced hushed whispers in my ear asking yes or yes questions
Courage cowered in the presence of their voices
My own voice went hoarse when I wanted to say stop, made me feel like a chicken
Shame from being goaded while pounded
Turned me sheepish
Eventually, I decided the buck stopped with me

Learned to count on my own voice
even though it was stolen from me before I knew what it sounded like
Now, I speak up for those who can't

Definitions from "Dedication to My Baby Girl"

PTSD=   the acronym for post-traumatic stress disorder which
             is a disorder in which a person has difficulty recovering
             after experiencing or witnessing a terrifying event.
             If you are still having problems 6 months after the event,
             more than likely, you are experiencing PTSD.

spawning=   of a fish, frog, crustacean, etc. Release or deposit eggs

perpetually= in a way that never ends or changes, constantly

coerced=   persuade an unwilling person to do something by using
             force or threats

cowered=   crouch down in fear

goaded=   to provoke or annoy someone so as to stimulate some action
             or reaction

Commentary from "Dedication to My Baby Girl"

Every rape or sexual assault isn't violent as far as being overly aggressive, including beatings and excessive physical force that leaves you with visible bruises. Nevertheless, rape and sexual assault is a violent act. Brianna Chenault explains, "At the time, I saw my power trapped behind their eyes every time I closed mine/ Body still violated though the violation wasn't violent/ Just silent and coerced / Hushed whispers in my ear asking yes or yes questions." Rape and sexual assault are about control and power. You have the right to say no at any time, even during an act that you consented to. No means no!

Violated
By TeMasi Love

(Themes: Incest & Rape)

If I could switch out my violator, would I feel less violated?
Because I'm tired.
Tired of the constant reminder of what is,
but what should've never been.
No matter how many times I try to erase that night,
the memories, they haunt me.
You….
Of all people, YOU!
I remember all the times I waited at the door
for you to pick me up as a young girl,
but you never did.
Many nights I cried myself to sleep before I closed my eyelids.
I thought…
Something must be wrong with me!
But those tears?
They were nothing compared to the ones from that night.
How could an innocent night out with you turn into a night of agony and regret?
Disgusted is an understatement, and now I am left broken and distressed.
Have you ever screamed for God to save you and heard nothing in return?
Am I to blame?!
Days turned into weeks, and weeks turned into months.
Before I knew it, I found myself sitting by a river.
Full of tears.
Full of questions.
Defeated.
Hurt.
Confused.
The water looked so pretty!!
It called out to me like the ocean called out to Moana.
But unlike her, I can't swim.

So, my fate rested on my decision to indulge in that calling.

Contemplating, I reminded myself that I have two reasons to live.

And on my phone a gentle voice said, "Don't let the Devil win!"

Thank God for life!

So, yes!

If I could switch out my violator, it might have been easier to make it through.

But because it's you I see when I look in the mirror…

I realize that I have some deep healing to do!

Commentary for "Violated"

Incest is rape that occurs between close relatives: daughters/sons and mothers or fathers, among cousins, sisters and brothers, etc. It takes a sick person to rape, sexual assault, or molest anyone, **ESPECIALLY** their own child! The topic of incest is avoided and very underreported to the authorities.

FIGURE 1
MANIFESTATIONS OF CHILDHOOD INCEST IN UNTREATED ADULTS

- Depression

- Low self-esteem

- Sexual dysfunction

- Feelings of powerlessness

- Lack of trust

- Compulsive disorders

- Impulsivity

- Self-destructive behavior

- Difficulty in parenting

- Difficulty in relationships

Body Bag
Rebecca Hollie Woods (aka Murder She Wrote)
(Themes: Domestic Violence & Physical Abuse)

My heart was racing,

Because I see him pacing

I could feel his rage

I knew what happened when he pumped his fist

Those rosy red cheeks

Were only a sign of what was to come

I wondered...what have I done?

I go through the anxiety of playing the blame game

Every time it was always the same

I was watching him from my truck,

Because of the fear I was stuck

Then, I saw him coming

Like a lion coming in for the kill

Before I could move, there he stood, he grabbed my hair

I fought with all my will

But his strength was overpowering and before I knew it

I felt him drag me out and over the gravel

Up the stairs in the house...all while pulling me by my hair

I remember fighting

Like a tumble weed in the desert

We were rolling around,

But then I felt that punch to the side of my ear

I could see his mouth moving

But I couldn't hear

Everything went black

I could feel myself going in and out

Finally, the pain brought me back

No time to think about why I was slain

He was gone...nowhere to be found

So I tried to rise without making a sound

Finally, I saw the lights

Red and blue, flashing

Now, I can feel my heart beat

I hear them come in

But so scared that it was him

I stayed were I was

Closed my eyes

Too scared that this moment would be my **demise**

Then, suddenly it hits me, where are my babies?

Somehow their little faces brought me back

I got to fight…I got to stand…I got to get to them

Hold their hands, let them know mommy's okay

I heard their little cries

Those little cries saved our lives

Later, after everything was over

My babies were okay

The detective came to my hospital room

He said I was safe...he wouldn't hurt me, today

But he couldn't leave until I heard what he needed to say

Your husband threw you through a wall

So I cannot sit here and stall

You need to know the **ramifications** of his actions

You need to know, we have him now

But he will eventually get out

Before that outline on the wall

Becomes an outline in the hall

You need to pack a bag and leave

I know your life is all up in the air...I know it seems like more than you can bare

Then, he looked at me with this long stare

I've seen this a million times

Too many women have met their demise

So make your decision now

Do not lag, take your final bag

If you listen to his lies and give him alibies,

You will leave this house again,

But next time in a body bag

Definitions for "Body Bag"

demise=   a person's death

ramifications= a consequence of an action or event, especially when complex
                or unwelcome

Commentary for "Body Bag"

As with the workshop I teach, the "Progression of Violence," domestic violence has a natural progression to become more and more violent. The level of aggression intensifies. The verbal assaults get more and more hurtful until you feel like you are dealing with it daily. The physical attacks get more frequent and the type of damage, emotionally and physically, increases overtime. Sometimes this happens gradually, but sometimes there are extreme increases in occurrence. Therefore, when you think of domestic violence, you can't say, "It was just one time." That one time leads to the next time, and the next time may be your last time. For more information on the "Progression of Violence" workshop, please contact MoPoetry Phillips via email at mopoetry@artsequitycollective.org.

The Shame Game
By Krista Coleman

(Theme: Shame)

Shame runs everything around me.

My actions are controlled by this little thought,

impulse that's says don't you dare.

Like Voldemort, I can't speak it, can't breathe it, better not show it.

What will people think when they find out your shame?

What about when they find out you are ashamed?

Shame is like a curse word.

A slur that shouldn't be talked about in mixed company,

or really any company.

It's a secret for you alone,

to hide somewhere in the corners of your soul.

To trap behind a cage, drop down a well,

barricade behind a Great Wall but never let it out.

When it tries to break out that cage, scale that wall and step a toe outside,

you must shove it back down.

Because the potential ramifications are tremendous enough

to bring on a full typhoon of worry and guilt.

No, shame cannot see the light of day.

You're not even supposed to possess it,

but now that you do, you need to hide it away.

Do not let the shame monster out of its cage.

Just let it dig at the ground of your soul

Scavenging at your self-esteem to chew upon.

Pour it a tall glass of your spirit, enthusiasm, and ambition.

Until you're drained, empty

When others start picking the scab shame left,

just redirect them to something superficial

and distracting like your new shoes you bought,

or something funny your cat did.

Don't give in. It's too dangerous.

And if you forget, just remember the last time you let shame out.

It multiplied in size in the span of seconds.

It evolved, **metamorphosed** into worry, then guilt,
then **self-loathing,** and finally **despair**.
There's no weapon against despair.
It puts you in a hold you can't escape,
cutting off circulation until you are numb.
Unable to move out of bed, unable to shower, eat, or work.
But shame is not yet done!
Now that you are in a vegetable state,
shame will feed upon you like leftovers from the night before.
Reminding you this is what happens when you let shame run the game.

Definitions for "The Shame Game"

Voldermort= a villain in the Harry Potter series

ramifications= a consequence of an action or event, especially when complex or unwelcome

typhoon= a tropical storm in the region of the Indian or western Pacific Ocean

scavenging= to collect anything usable from discarded waste

enthusiasm= a strong feeling of excitement, interest, or eagerness

ambition= a strong desire to do or to achieve something, typically requiring determination and hard work

superficial= existing or occurring at or on the surface

metamorphosed=the process of transformation from a mature form to an adult form in two or more distinct states, normally speaks of an insect or amphibians

self-loathing= also known as self-hatred, refers to intense feelings of disliking oneself. When a person shows persistent self-criticism and a belief that they are not worthy or undeserving

despair= the complete loss or absence of hope

Commentary for "The Shame Game"

Look at the "Symptoms of Guilt vs. Shame" image below by Oro House Recovery. Then, consider this. If I was coughing uncontrollably, what are some reasons that I might cough? Did you say asthma.. allergies… a cold… Covid? (Hopefully, not). The cough is only the symptom, but it is important to find out the disease, or root cause. It is the same way when we have guilt and shame. It is important to find out why those feelings exist. It may require you to go back to things in your childhood, things you know are unresolved in your life, or areas of pain you don't like to admit. Dealing with the shame requires healing.

Symptoms of Guilt vs Shame

Guilt
- Regret from bad behavior
- Anxiety
- Ruminating about the past
- Apologizing for harm
- Desiring to do better

Shame
- Feeling worthless
- Low self-esteem
- Anger issues
- Using drugs & alcohol
- Hiding or isolating

Earth-Shattering
By Krista Coleman

(Theme: Anxiety)

I'm so wound up with anxiety
it's wrapped me up in a strait jacket
of my own making
Constricting every thought,
emotion, word, expression
Nothing escapes
Bound around my chest
unable to gasp
or release an exhale
Suffocating, choking on trauma
Trembling with fear that I might explode-
all of it on my family and peers
An earthquake shakes the foundation of my being,
and I can't sit still
I grab at anything nearby that may save me
from a bloody fate
But the ground splits open beneath me
With a precision knife a burst of exhaustion teams from the soil
and works its way up the surface of my eventual repose.
The calm after the storm-
surveying what needs to be repurposed, repaired,
and rinsed of the confirmation
Plaster over the evidence there ever was a storm.
Repaint. Reglaze and Make like new.
Until the next storm

Definitions for "Earth-Shattering
constricting=   make narrower, especially by applying outside
                 pressure around it
repose=   a state of rest, sleep, or tranquility
repurposed=   adapt for use in a different purpose

Commentary for "Earth-Shattering"

Actual earthquakes and earth-shattering things that happen in our lives are both destructive just in different ways. Actual earthquakes can shift houses off their foundations; tear roofs off and can literally cause total devastation. When we experience earth-shattering events, our Sympathetic Nervous System gets overly stimulated. Our bodies begin to release all kinds of stress hormones including adrenaline, cortisol, and norepinephrine. We are thrown into a trauma response which could be fight, flight, freeze, and fawn. The only way to alleviate this is to stimulate the Parasympathetic Nervous System.

Activity

List five things that can stimulate the Parasympathetic Nervous System.

 **SYMPATHETIC NERVOUS SYSTEM**

 **PARASYMPATHETIC NERVOUS SYSTEM**

Stress Response
Revs you up, preparing you to fight, take flight or freeze

- Heart beats fast
- Breath is fast and shallow
- Pupils of eyes expand (can make you sensitive to light)
- Gut becomes inactive (difficult to digest)
- Blood rushes to your skeletal muscles and away from your brain, making it hard to think clearly
- Hormones rush through your body, making you feel anxious
- Expends your energy

Relaxation Response
Calms you down, preparing you to rest, think and restore

- Heart beats in slow, rhythmic pattern
- Breath is full and slow
- Pupils of the eyes shrink
- Gut is active (helps you digest and absorb the nutrients from your food)
- Increased blood flow to gut, lungs and brain
- Hormones rush in, lifting your mood and helping you to relax
- Conserves your energy

 Zensational Kids

Intrusive
By Krista Coleman

(Themes: Intrusive Thoughts & Silence)

I feel it in my chest first,

That something to be unnamed,

Because if you name it, it makes it real.

So, when I feel it start to thump just beneath my ribcage,

I empty my mind to a vacuum that holds a simmering silence.

It bubbles up to my throat and catches my voice.

"What's wrong?"

"Want to talk about it?"

They don't know there's an invisible noose constricting my windpipe.

It's holding down that something inside my belly.

It's warm, and aching, and makes my mouth contort into ugly sneers.

My mind mired in mutilated memories,

Tortured into watching my own documentaries

Featuring a girl who knew no better,

Making decisions that will last forever.

Stifling any chance at future romance,

Because she cannot let go of the nightmarish dance.

Who knew that bruises and cuts made in 2010

Would purple and scab for years on end.

Definitions for "Intrusive"

intrusive thoughts=	unwanted, involuntary, and disturbing thoughts, images, or urges that can appear suddenly. They can be scary, offensive or shameful and may contradict a person's values or beliefs.
noose=	is a loop at the end of a rope or wire that is tied with a knot allowing it to tighten when pulled
constricting=	make narrower, especially by applying outside pressure around it
sneers=	displaying an expression or utterance of disrespect
mired=	cause to become stuck in mud
mutilated=	inflict a violent or disfiguring injury on
stifling=	very hot or causing difficulties in breathing

Commentary for "Intrusive"

Seeing so many young people and adults suffer in silence is the constant motivator for the work I do with survivors. Silence delays healing and inflicts additional wounds. Silence is a good actor and plays the role of protector while causing harm. Silence can fester or becomes more problematic over time as shame and false guilt, and may manifest as physical sickness, mental illness, and drug and alcohol use.

I'm Not Your Victim: I Am Free
By Megan Johnston

(Themes: Empowerment, Rape, & Unprotected Victims)

You may have tried to hurt me and tried to cut me down.
Days of constant jokes, always at my expense.
Nights I lie awake, hoping it would change.
Treating me as your own toy for torment.

The days I tried to get help, but that came far too late.
The night you tried to rape me,
And the day I wasn't believed.
The sleepless nights I wake,
wondering what I did.
Why did they believe your lies?

You may have tried to break me,
but this moment won't define;
I'm moving on from this pain
Getting stronger every day;
Letting go of all the anger, sadness.
No more tears, you have no power over me.

Your voice inside my head is quickly fading
I won't listen to you now.
You are not worth an ounce of thought
and definitely not worth my time.
My life is mine to make, chasing dreams I thought were gone.
Living truly for me
Becoming who I am, and who I want to be,
C'est mon vie!!
Je suis libre!

Definitions for "I'm Not Your Victim: I Am Free"
C'est mon vie!!=   French for "That's my life!"
Je suis libre!=   French for "I am free"

Commentary for "I'm Not Your Victim: I Am Free"

Megan speaks of "The night you **tried** to rape me." What a lot of people fail to realize is that even when a person doesn't successfully complete the entire physical violation, there is still an emotional violation and hurt that impacts his/hers/their victim. I sarcastically call these incidents "near misses," because it almost missed, but it didn't. If you have ever experienced a person looking at you inappropriately, seducing you into inappropriate conversations, or even making you feel uncomfortable in any way, know that what they have done is betray your trust, and made you feel unsafe.

How Hurt is this World
By Megan Johnston

(Theme: Community Responsibility)

How hurt is our world that stories go unspoken

Stories go unheard

Listened to, but not believed

How hurt is our world that we let others suffer

Waiting in the intersection of action and inaction

Waiting for assistance, agency, support

a kind word, a supportive shoulder

hoping to ease the pain;

To not walk this road alone.

Hoping, praying no one else goes through this too!

Pain on pain, it multiplies

Hurt on hurt, we spin

How hurt is our world?

Sitting at a football game

A woman says to her friend

I'll watch your back you watch mine

It's echoed by her daughter to her friend

Fear passed generation to generation

How hurt is our world?

That the echo of boys will be boys

Or they would never do that

Or they have a bright future, it was one mistake,

Rings louder than the cries for help

The echo of the unnoticed

What about them

How hurt is our world?

What about *their* future?

They are left to pick up the pieces

Asked why they aren't better

What did they themselves do, or did, or didn't do

How hurt is our world?
They bear the pain
The others move on
*Oh, how hurt is **this** world.*

Commentary for "How Hurt is This World"

Looking at what is going on in the world can be depressing. But no matter what happens, we have a responsibility as a community to advocate for justice, demand equality, stand in unison for fair treatment, and speak out against anything that tries to destroy us as a people.

Un-dropped Tears
By Megan Johnston

(Theme: Healing)

They tell you, "Be strong,
Don't let them see your pain."

The pain now thrust inside
Enveloping your **authentic** self
The one you **scurry** away
Whenever someone might hurt you again,
Un-dropped tears tearing inside you,
Weighing on your soul weathered with a salty stain
Preserving the pain pressured under the present
Festering in the now **fragile** future
Keeping you trapped under its torment.

Tearing at the **construct** while trying to break free,
Until it snaps, soothing the ache underneath
As tears escape easing the pain and torment
Eroding the mask you once wore,
Revealing the hidden gem now glowing in the light.
Cleansed from the pain and restored to life.

Definitions for "Un-dropped Tears"

enveloping=   to wrap up, cover, or surround completely
authentic=   of undisputed origin, genuine
scurry=   move hurriedly with short, quick steps
festering=   of a wound or sore forming puss, septic
fragile=   easily broken or damaged
construct=   something constructed by the mind such as a theoretical
                entity, a working concept, or a product of
                ideology, history, or social circumstance

Commentary for "Un-dropped Tears"

No matter who you are it is ok to cry. Look below for the "Reasons Why Crying is Good."

REASONS WHY CRYING IS GOOD

It shows us that something is wrong.

It removes toxins from the body

Enhances mood and improves vision.

Helps you let go of bottled up emotions.

Helps you sleep better.

It releases stress hormones

Helps you recover from grief.

Regulates emotions and calms you down.

Helps others understand that you need support.

Helps to relieve both emotional and physical pain.

Innsightful
@innsightful_

Our Brother Starred as Seaweed in the Senior Musical
By NitaJade

(Theme: Autism)

& my sister paints Black women into trees

& my mother fills her journals with memoir

& my bestie fights for Black kids on **spectrums**

& my mentor tours national parks with grandkids

& my mentor wraps buildings in poetry

& my mentor **cooks portals to ancestors**

& my mentor writes us lethal when bound

& my cousin organizes love for her mother

& my little cousin installs lashes & plays ball

& my grandmother shimmied after tasting a new dish

& my great-grandmother spent her last breaths in song

& (since he's really your brother, too), our brother played the role,

became Seaweed, sang   *I can't see why people look at me & only see the color*
of my face.   He practiced for weeks (didn't he?) to get the   *only*   just right.

Definitions for "Our Brother Starred as Seaweed in the Senior Musical"

spectrums=   typically means to be diagnosed with
                                     Autism Spectrum Disorder (ASD)

cooked portals to ancestors= refers to someone cooking as a way to connect
                                     with your heritage and family traditions

Commentary for "Our Brother Starred as Seaweed in the Senior Musical"

Many children and adults on the autism spectrum aren't understood. They face bias and are discriminated against. They call it a spectrum, because there are various symptoms and ranges of impact. While some are greatly impacted, others may be on the spectrum who are slightly impacted. Some of the symptoms of autism are difficulty communicating, being sensitive to loud noises, avoiding eye contact and touch, preferring to play alone, tiptoeing, displaying loud outbursts, repetitive body behaviors known as "stimming", and being unaware of potential dangers. However, as the chart below shows, there are several positive characteristics of being autistic as well.

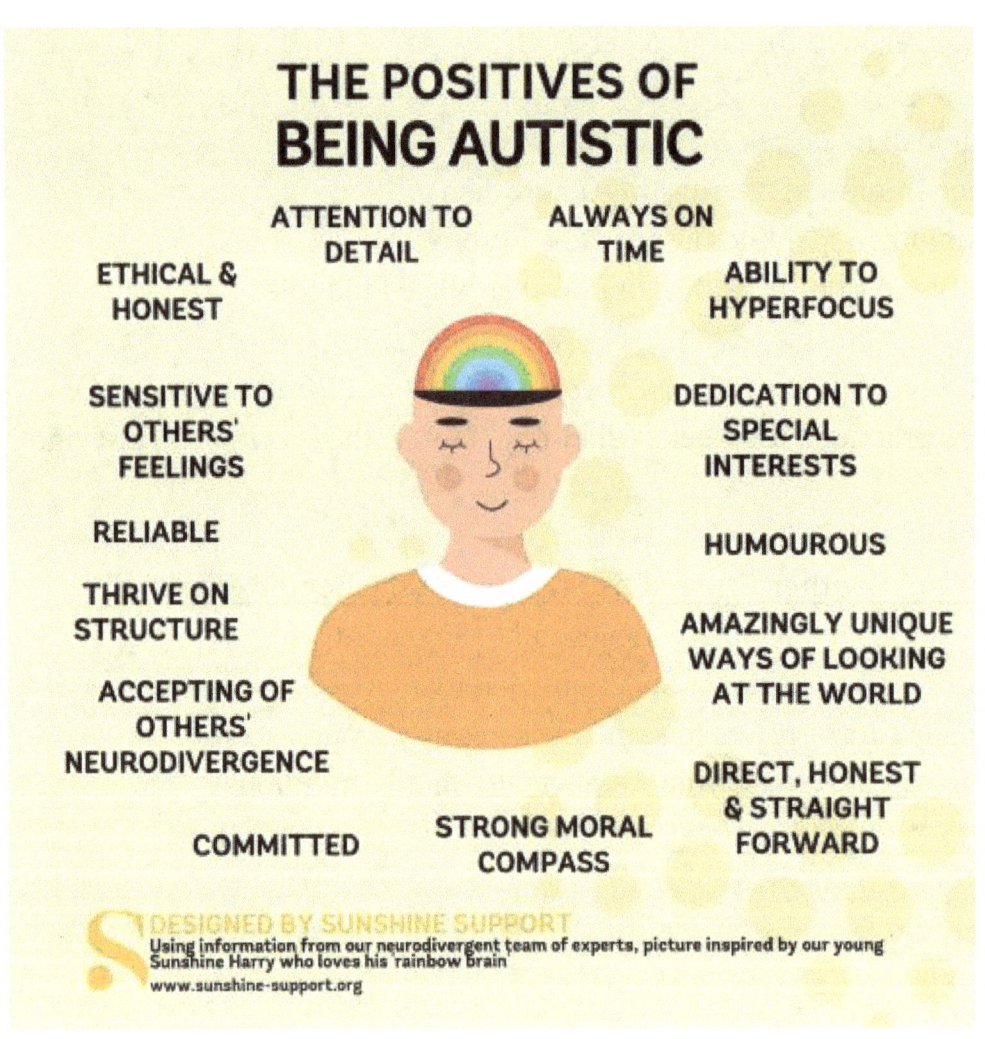

Dear Abuser
By Beth Warren

(Themes: Domestic Violence, Physical Abuse, & Mental Abuse)

Dear Abuser, she writes, as she picks the broken pieces up, that lay scattered across the floor. Pieces of her **carousel**, the painted one she hid behind the door.

I'm sorry for yelling she cries; you are the one that I adore. She writes about the anger she feels, to talk and talk but still be ignored. She always says, "I'm sorry," even though I repeatedly come back for more.

Is there no justice in this world or is someone somehow **incessantly** keeping score? One point for him, because he doesn't scream in her face anymore. Two points for him, after he cleans all the blood off the floor. One point taken from her, because she woke the baby, screaming I hate you and wish you were never born.

Dear Abuser, she writes, hands bleeding from the glass thrown at the door. I'm sorry I got so angry that I pressed the gas to the floor. I just don't know how to live in this place with you anymore.

She wipes her tears with his shirt, but they keep falling to the floor. Despite the pain she feels throughout her body, it's her heart that's really sore. Her recognition of their broken marriage was just too much for her to endure.

Definitions for "Dear Abuser"

carousel=   a merry go round
incessantly= without interruption, constantly

Commentary for "Dear Abuser"

As difficult as it is to understand, it is possible that two seemingly conflicting things can be true:

1) A victim knew they were right to leave an abusive relationship.
2) A victim can be disappointed that their marriage, or relationship has come to an end.

The best way to heal is to find safety, security, and stability. Focus on rebuilding your family, friendships, enjoying life, and making new memories.

Dear Self
By Nicole (last name unknown)

(Themes: Recovery & Encouragement)

Dear Self;

You have come so far,
Fought so hard and are almost free!
As you leave the struggles of addiction in the past,
be kinder to yourself in RECOVERY!
You are a warrior,
and a child of God!
You have the blood of a KING in your veins!
You are sweet, funny, love animals,
root for the underdog,
and you are nice to everyone!
Start including yourself!
Forgive yourself for the pain
you have caused and forgive yourself!
You have walked a million painful miles in these shoes!
Time to trade them in for a new pair
to walk this road called RECOVERY!
But, keep the old pair to remember your journey
and a compass in case a speed bump makes you lose your way!

Commentary for "Dear Self"

Use the picture below as a prompt to write your version of "Dear Self."
Learning to encourage yourself is a wonderful gift.

Today
Rebecca Hollie Woods (aka Murder She Wrote)
(Themes: Empowerment & Encouragement)

Today, I put on a skirt
And let the music hit my soul
I danced like I had full control
Control of every movement
Steps coordinated for every beat
Pointed toes and light feet
I danced like no one was watching
I took a deep breath
I introduced sunshine to my lungs
It shined so bright
Throughout my body
Arms reaching out to the heavens
And I think my laced fingertips could reach the blue in the sky
I was just trying to get closer to you
I embraced this moment
I enjoyed the warmth of the sun
Then, I realized it was you
I felt your arms wrap around me
And embrace me
Today… I allowed myself to feel your love
I allowed myself the forgiveness to accept…what I deserve
Today …I gave myself permission to step out of reserve
And feel you
Today, I felt each stretch and each turn
And it didn't hurt
I went to take a breath
And I could feel the air
My skin did not burn
Today…I was not followed by a cloud of doubt
The skies were clear
I could see where I was going

When you carried me
I floated in the air
Gracefully
No apologies are needed
For my energy
Because the only one that needs to keep up
Is me
Thank you for the time
To stand in your light
And shine, because…
Today, I loved me…unapologetically

Commentary for "Today"

SOS Empowerment Arts & Healing by Arts Equity Collective (A Book of Poetry & Visual Arts About Survivors' Stories) creates a safe and supportive environment for survivors of mental, physical, and emotional trauma, where they can process their pain through creative expression. However, the purpose is to use those stories to educate young adults, empower them, and help them heal. As the author above encourages, I just ask you to love yourself unapologetically. Use these tools to help you throughout your healing journey.

Index (Themes: Page Numbers)